A.E.V. Oliver

KRIEGIE

GEORGE MANN *of* MAIDSTONE

KRIEGIE
by A.E.V. Oliver

First Published by George Mann Books 1998

Printed and bound in the United Kingdom
by MFP Design and Print, Manchester
and published by
George Mann Books, PO Box 22
Maidstone
in the English County of Kent

KRIEGIE

Contents

1

In the beginning

ON THAT SULTRY SATURDAY EVENING of September 2nd 1939, the High Life went on as usual in Trinidad's Port of Spain. Fleets of sleek hired limousines deposited gaggles of excited party goers on the columned steps of the Country Club before purring off into the warm night to pick up more. The men were resplendent in their white tuxedos, the ladies scintillated in their finery, groomed and bejewelled to perfection, as they flitted and flirted here and there at the entrance, like moths attracted to the bright colourful lights illuminating the bougainvillaea, hibiscus and other tropical flora, which cascaded in wild profusion from under the stately palms lining the avenue to the club.

It was an intoxicating scene. The full moon cast a silvery light everywhere, filtering brightly through the glistening fronds of the coconut palms. The air was heavily scented by frangipani blossoms and filled with the sound of cicadas and croaking frogs, while myriads of fireflies flitted in suspended animation like millions of earthbound stars to complete nature's pageant of the night. It all signalled the beginning of just another Saturday night's revelry at the club where, under the patronage of the English Governor and his Lady, the 'bright young things' of the Colony let down their hair to the accompaniment of calypso music, spurred on by the copious consumption of rum, not always diluted with coca-cola.

In the early hours of Sunday, the Governor's entourage would leave to a dramatic and sudden rendition of the National Anthem, the ADC surreptitiously ensuring that any remains of the Duty Free Scotch which had graced their privileged table were taken back to Government House. That was the signal for the dancing to stop. Soon everyone was wishing everyone else a fervent goodbye, even though, after a few hours sleep, many of them would greet each other again even more enthusiastically, round the bandstand in the grounds of Government House where every Sunday the Police band played more sedate music.

Everybody who was anybody in the social world bade goodbye to their friends, especially those who had travelled from San Fernando some forty-five miles south where they were employed in the bush on the various oil fields owned by international companies. To them Saturday nights were their only real opportunity to taste the joys of civilisation.

Most eligible young males on the island, apart from those born into the more affluent local families, were of English extraction and engaged in Accountancy, Banking, Insurance, Commerce or in Oil production, complemented by young officers from the Police and the British forces. Germany provided a suspiciously large contingent of expatriates, considering its small diplomatic and commercial interest, but the young men of all nations mixed well in every walk of life and indeed were good friends, although the Germans never completely dropped their air of teutonic superiority.

That particular Saturday night our German friends

appeared less at ease than usual and left earlier. Little did they know that at the Club that evening they were being kept under close surveillance by Major Morgan and his colonial Police Officers. They must have been very surprised when they were detained next day on a beach at Cocorite, where they had surreptitiously organised a boat to take them under cover of darkness to neighbouring Venezuela.

A few hours later, as we were playing our usual Sunday morning round of golf, an army dispatch rider raced up to the club house at Maraval at high speed to confirm what until then we had only guessed was coming: that England and Germany were now at war.

Within a few days, with the enthusiasm of youth, I had decided to resign my job with Barclays Bank (Dominion Colonial and Overseas) and was on my way by ship to England via the USA to volunteer for service in the Royal Air Force where I had ambitions of becoming a pilot. So it was goodbye to all my friends in paradise! I had grown to love life on that tropical island, the warmth generated not only by its lively friendly people, but by the glorious sun which warmed its seas and its beaches and set nature alight. I just hoped that I would return!

If you had eaten of the special local Trinidadian dish 'saltfish and akee', it was prophesied that you would and I had devoured that magical dish many times with relish. Trinidad had been a dream I would never forget, where the warm-hearted people had accepted me so generously as part of their family groups.

When I arrived in England, however, I found that in sharp contrast, life was grim, cold and grey. At night the whole country was under a total blackout - even car headlights were by law fitted with special grilles to severely dim them down. Food was rationed, clothes and petrol too. A small bedsit in London in Russell Square stretched my financial resources to the limit as I was then unemployed. At the Air Ministry there was more gloom. My chances of being selected for pilot training were nil. England had more trained pilots than aircraft, although the numbers of both were woefully short of its needs.

By haunting the corridors of the Air Ministry daily and embarrassing the recruiting staff with stories of my impending bankruptcy, I was informed eventually that the Government proposed to recruit eight hundred Air Gunner Officers for some new Bomber Command strategy and I was invited to apply for selection. To my great relief I was commissioned into the RAF.

It was on my twenty-ninth birthday, December 30th 1939, that I was instructed to report to RAF Aldergrove in Northern Ireland as an acting pilot officer. It had been snowing hard. In places, drifts were twenty feet deep and it was bitterly cold as well as blowing a blizzard. However I was now in the Services, where orders were orders, and I was naive enough to believe that if I did not report to Aldergrove on time it could seriously affect the course of the war!

Transport was chaotic and a naval vessel had been specially commissioned to move service personnel from Liverpool to Belfast. The journey from Belfast by train to Aldergrove village was tortuous, but paled into insignificance when compared with the trip from Aldergrove's deserted railway station to the airfield. Normally, service transport would have been available, but as the road was completely impassable and telephone lines were down everywhere it was necessary for me to wade through the deep snowdrifts carrying my large cabin trunk, 'coolie-like' on my head, drenched and blinded by the blizzard which was still raging.

Against all the odds, finally presenting myself at the camp was an herculean achievement which I was proud to have accomplished so early in my RAF career, although I was suffering total exhaustion. Imagine my chagrin when I staggered wet and bedraggled into the Adjutant's office to be greeted with the news that I was not expected, as no signal of my posting had been received! I could not be allowed to take up residence in the Officers' Mess until notice of my posting had been verified, so I was provisionally accommodated some five miles away in a fairly basic unheated hotel room in Antrim until conditions returned to normal.

Subsequently over a period of seven weeks at Aldergrove, under continual harassment from Republican terrorists who sniped at us around the airfield and when we drove about the area in the evenings, twenty-five raw recruits were licked into shape as officer air gunners. Consequently, I found myself, after a few further weeks at various stations in England, transported to France as a full blown Pilot Officer.

Our Fairey Battles had been fashioned with the same desperation as had the flying crews which manned them. The Germans had to be stopped at all costs. The planes were quite incapable of standing up to the German fighters. They were slow and cumbersome with so little effective fire power that we were sitting ducks. We were quite literally shot out of the skies. Many of my friends lost their lives in those few dark days before Dunkirk, when Britain was forced to evacuate her forces from Europe.

I survived, by boarding a small ship, dressed only in my flying gear, as the few planes still airborne were used to scramble off more senior officers. I was expendable as far as the RAF was concerned. It was a matter of *suave qui peut.*

Back in England there followed attachments to night bomber squadrons, first to No. 78 at Linton-on-Ouse in Yorkshire and then to Dishforth and Leeming with No. 10 Squadron, equipped with Whitleys. Made by Armstrong Whitworth, the Whitley bomber was a pencil-like plane powered by two Rolls Royce Merlin engines, similar to those deployed in Spitfires. It was fitted with a Fraser Nash power operated 4-gun turret in the tail which was my cold and inhospitable roost while on operations. In flight the planes flew distinctively, nose-down, but we liked our Rolls Royce engines and the German fighters didn't like those power operated turrets, so it was only necessary to fire in short sharp bursts to keep them at bay.

May onwards, our night bombing missions took us over the Ruhr, the German industrial heartland, to such well defended targets as Mannheim, Dusseldorf and Duisberg. Most of these raids resulted in heavy casualties and provided many exciting moments for the survivors. I was anxious to push up my number of operations to the magical total of twenty-one trips since, being Gunnery Leader of 'A' Flight in 10 Squadron, I was aware that it was likely I would be awarded a DFC if I survived that long!

I very much coveted that DFC. But it was not to be.

2

Downed!

DURING MY SEVEN MONTHS IN THE RAF I had settled down to enjoy an exciting time on Operations. Days were enlivened by close relationships with fellow officers and nights spiced with the company of lovely WAAF girlfriends when I wasn't flying.

Ever present, always there, providing a shock of sudden fear sometimes and always the thrill of danger were the Operations themselves.

Nevertheless, you always had the deep down basic feeling that you were immortal. It was always the other fellow who bought it.

Wasn't it?

Little did I realise that the dawn of August 15th 1940 was to signal the beginning of a very different chapter in my life.

That morning I was stretched lazily between the sheets in my bachelor quarters in an over-large red brick house on the edge of the airfield at the operational bomber station, RAF Leeming in Yorkshire. The house had been built to provide accommodation for a Wing Commander in peacetime and other houses of greater or lesser pretensions were located at discreet distances from each other, each appropriate in size to the rank of the peacetime occupier.

In wartime, service families had been evacuated from operational stations, so the houses were used, room by room, as makeshift quarters for the young officer aircrew.

All officers dined in the adjacent Officers' Mess, an imposing rambling building, and used the commodious lounges and bars as a very comfortable club, open day and night. The building had also been well able to provide adequate living quarters for all unmarried officers in peacetime, but was now only able to provide sleeping accommodation for the most senior.

Sleeping outside the Mess had distinct advantages for the younger officer. All kinds of assignations could be arranged, far away from the censorious eyes of straitlaced senior staff.

10 Squadron had only been at Leeming a short while, having been transferred there from Dishforth a few miles down the A1. Such transfers were never popular for, although everybody attached to squadron operations moved en-bloc, the move meant parting from cosy, warm, even intimate relationships with the previous station's permanent staff, including many beautiful young WAAFs.

As I lay there in bed that morning I realised how fortunate I had been in my short time at Leeming. I had made a conquest, a young WAAF just five years younger than my twenty-nine years. She was beautiful, tall and blonde, just a slip of a girl almost ethereal, as she glided into my life in her form fitting uniform. I fully realised how lucky I was that somebody so beautiful and caring had come my way just at that time.

I was young enough not to doubt that I might be considered attractive to the opposite sex, particularly as the patriotic wartime press gave all aircrew a dashing, glamorous image, but nonetheless I considered myself particularly fortunate.

At almost the same time as the Squadron had arrived at Leeming, Dianne had been posted in to be the station commander's personal driver. This position gave her unique status amongst her fellow WAAFs who were a little jealous of the good looks and personality which had singled her out for this prestigious appointment.

It was the custom of the commanding officer to have her drive him around various dispersal points on the perimeter of the airfield when the dispersal vans were dropping the crews by their planes before takeoff on the night's raid. The CO's car moved swiftly from plane to plane trundling up in the dusk to the end of the runway where they were given a friendly wave and wished 'bon voyage'.

My position in the rear turret gave me a clear view of the two remote figures in the descending twilight, watching and waving as my aircraft lumbered up the runway and hauled itself up into the darkening sky. To me there was only one person waving and she was not the CO's driver. She was Dianne, my girlfriend, and her waving always appeared to be very intimate and urgent.

Neither one of us had ever admitted to the other that they had at any time wondered if that wave was ever to be a final farewell. Farewell and goodbye forever to all we had come to mean to each other and which we had physically expressed as recently as the night before. It had become a ritual, waving goodbye at the edge of the airfield and never questioning that we would be reunited.

In this state of limbo the relationship flourished blissfully. That it was too good to last never entered our heads. But fate now took a hand.

My Squadron Leader tipped me off that the Station Commander had become aware of my relationship with his driver and didn't like it. It was like a bolt from the blue. I had no idea that he had designs on my girlfriend. No Group Captain in command of a bomber station would tolerate one of his junior officers encroaching on his preserves. The Group Captain had personally selected this lady to be his driver, and he had apparently decided to make her his own personal wartime property.

He might have forgiven a junior officer casting admiring glances at his wife or even paying her court, but his beautiful driver was definitely off limits. She was his perk. In these circumstances the law of the jungle applied - the most powerful prevailed - he was supreme and no young cub could sneak up and snatch the prize. The penalty for trying was ostracism from the pack and that was what I could expect. The Group Captain could instruct the Squadron Leader to have me posted to another squadron, no trouble. There was a constant need to reshuffle airgunners as they had a low survival rate on operations.

I could see there were going to be problems ahead.

I was aroused from my reverie by my WAAF batman bringing in my early morning cup of tea. She was a plain, cheerful almost motherly girl, who saw to it that my clothes were always in good order and repair and that my sleeping quarters were kept scrupulously clean and tidy. She was a marvellously cheerful girl but, needless to say, I had none of the proprietary feelings towards my aide that the Station Commander apparently had towards his.

In leisurely fashion, I had breakfast in the Mess and then strolled down to the flights with my friends for briefing on the coming night's operations. We all knew we were flying that night but it came as a complete surprise when we were told that the target was a new one and not Germany as usual.

We were going to hit Italy. The Squadron was to be deployed on a raid on the Fiat works in Turin where aero engines were being manufactured. Some two months earlier, with the collapse of France and the B.E.F.'s forced retreat from Dunkirk, the Italians had judged it safe to enter the war on what they believed would be the winning side. It was to be our job to demonstrate to them that they had made a big mistake.

At the same time, our crews were surprised that the target that night was to be Turin. Targets in Italy had so far been considered too remote for successful attack with Whitleys from bases in England. A Whitley bomber had a maximum operational ceiling of fifteen thousand feet, so it was obvious that a flight over the Alps was going to pose more problems than a strike over the North Sea, the Zuider Zee and the plains of Germany to targets in the industrial Ruhr.

Turin was tucked in like a limpet under the Alps with the sixteen thousand feet high snow capped peak of Mont Blanc barring the way.

It was going to be extremely difficult for planes heavily laden with bombs to reach the required height and then descend almost vertically down the Alps on the Italian side.

To add to these hazards the Germans had already located

many fighter squadrons throughout Occupied France with particularly strong concentrations around Paris and along the north French coast. As our heavy bomber squadrons were situated mainly in Lincolnshire and Yorkshire, aircraft had to be airborne for a round trip of approximately twelve hours, half of that time under full load, which put the plane and the crew under heavy stress.

At 3.00 pm on August 15th, 10 Squadron took off from Leeming for Abingdon where the aircraft would refuel to gain those extra few precious miles needed to carry out an operation of such duration. A trip to Germany was usually all over in six to seven hours.

Our arrival at Abingdon created a sensation. The station was a training centre and had never seen a bomber squadron in battle array. It had been impressed upon us that it was vitally important our destination was kept totally secret, to give German intelligence no chance to alert their fighter patrols just across the Channel. As the crews sat around in the Abingdon Mess waiting for dusk to fall, everyone was silent and preoccupied, just gazing at the posters and realising the significance of the warnings that 'walls have ears'.

At 9.00 pm the Squadron was airborne again and slipped across the Channel at Hastings. In the gathering dusk we reached the French coast to begin the long, tedious journey overland to Turin. Once clear of the French coast the German presence inland caused little concern. Here and there a probing searchlight half-heartedly questioned the presence of intruders, then quickly fell away. The air gunners kept up a watchful vigil for dreaded night fighters, knowing from past experience that when the searchlights opened up without accompanying anti-aircraft barrages, the probability was that fighters were aloft in the area, just waiting for the searchlights to pin-point the bombers for them.

Our aircraft droned on hour after hour, it seemed endless, but it was some comfort to the crews up in the vast blackness of the sky to know they were not alone, that the friends with whom they had been laughing and joking just a few hours before were riding the night sky with them, their senses keyed up to the same fever pitch, all bent on the same mission.

At the end of an eternity of switching the gun turret from beam to beam, upwards and downwards to ensure the security of the aircraft, a few straggling lights appeared faintly ahead. Never on previous trips had we seen such phenomena. In Germany and throughout the whole of occupied Europe blackout was total. Draconian fines were imposed on anyone infringing the regulations with even more ferocious penalties for repeated offences. So compliance was absolute. The lights ahead told us that we were passing from France into Switzerland, which had maintained neutrality, and came from unshuttered houses perched high in the mountains. Below lay Lake Geneva, a silver pool of reflected light, encircled with coloured fairy lights which confirmed that we were spot on in our navigation. Just across the Alps lay Turin!

Before leaving base the pilots had been instructed to use Lake Geneva as a marker beacon, a flagrant disregard of Swiss neutrality. Now Switzerland must show it was not prepared to have its neutrality violated with impunity. Searchlights began to probe the sky for the uninvited guests which direction finders had indicated were overhead. Anti-aircraft guns opened up, carefully ensuring they were all well off target, to avoid shooting down intruders who were only availing themselves of Swiss landmarks with no evil intent on the territory itself. A hit would have caused international embarrassment!

The snow which covered the ground far below now became clearly visible in the reflected light from the glistening peaks and appeared to be rushing up quickly to meet our plane, and despite the pilot's frantic efforts it was impossible to pull the machine up higher to clear Mont Blanc altogether.

The aircraft dipped, rose and shuddered as it struggled to gain height without success, while at the same time lurching forward and miraculously avoiding first one peak and then another like a drunken reveller on his way home in the blackout. Then suddenly the mountains which had threatened us so cruelly fell away beneath the plane as if sucked down by a gigantic vacuum cleaner. The Alps had been successfully negotiated and in a deep dark abyss beyond the mountain range lay the target.

To avoid detection by enemy defences it was necessary to descend quietly and in ever decreasing close spirals so as to position the aircraft directly over the target on the outskirts of the city.

The Italians had been completely taken by surprise. It was past midnight and lights still shone in the streets, where iridescent sparks marked the passage of tramcars. Down and down we spiralled, engines cut back to the merest whisper, falling silently and swiftly like some great eagle, down, ever down towards the oblivious prey.

In the light of the city it was possible to pick out the large sprawl of the Fiat works quite clearly. The concrete roofed area was used as a car testing track and presented a truly magnificent target.

Everything was peaceful, not even a solitary searchlight questioned the presence of raiders overhead, now levelling off for the short run-in to the target. It was not until the bombs from the leading aircraft had dropped that the city woke up to danger.

An explosion of dust and flame enveloped the factory area.

Then our own bombs had plunged away and, released from its load, our aircraft leapt upwards and, like a greyhound unleashed, throttles open, engines roaring, sped swiftly southwards over the dark countryside, circling once to survey the conflagration which appeared to be devouring the whole Fiat factory.

The crew was jubilant. So far, the mission had been entirely successful. The enemy had been caught completely off balance so that not a single salvo had been fired at us. Some Italian heads would roll in the morning when the extent of the damage had been assessed! Fires started by incendiary bombs from other aircraft were increasing in intensity, fountains of flame leaping skyward as chemicals and rubber compounds exploded. As we finished our circuit of the scene I treated the trams and cars below to a few short sharp bursts of machinegun fire which the front gunner echoed, but we were both very conscious of the vital need to conserve ammunition for probable skirmishes later. The night was still young and much could yet happen.

There was no need to court disaster by remaining longer

over the target area. The objective now was to regain height as quickly as possible to re-cross the Alps, and to get back to the comparative safety of the English Channel before dawn broke. The German fighters having been alerted to the fact that British bombers had broken through their defences to penetrate as far as Turin would be out to wreak their revenge on the returning raiders.

Our crews had ample experience of what to expect from previous trips over Germany. It was usually in the bright dawning of another day on their way back over France or Holland, tired and a little bedraggled after their encounters with the enemy, that they were intercepted by the German fighter patrols.

The fighters could often be seen in the distance glinting in the early morning sunlight, darting here and there like a swarm of hornets waiting to attack but frequently, and thankfully, there was some cloud cover below them and then the perfidious bombers would slam down their noses, dive into the safety of the clouds and not venture out again until they were well clear of the French coast.

The bombing of Turin was the thirtieth operation that our Skipper, Sergeant Pilot Green, had completed and, sitting anxiously at the controls, he put the Whitley into a series of spirals to climb to the height of sixteen thousand feet before re-crossing the Alpine range. Flying Officer Higson, the co-pilot, was manning the gun in the front nose turret, while Sergeant Millington, the navigator and Sergeant Davis the wireless operator were plotting the homeward course. The whole time the aircraft was climbing quickly, revelling in its lightened load.

Once over the Alps, the crew would still be keyed up as we crossed enemy territory, but thoughts of what lay ahead beyond the Channel, when we got home, would gradually intrude ever more and more strongly.

There'd be the sheer sense of relief when the wheels finally went down on the runway. That long pee over a tail-wheel. The first cup of coffee, cigarettes alight all around. Debriefing then back, pipe in hand, to the warmth of the Mess; rowdy greetings from other crews; and the excitement of shooting a line or telling the sober, hair-raising truth to each other over the eggs and bacon breakfast. Finally, plans would be hatched before they sought the sanctuary of their beds as to what they'd do that evening if, as they hoped, they would not be on Ops once again.

For the bachelors it would be a get-together in a local pub with their girlfriends, while to the married men it would mean relief for their wives who had spent yet another sleepless night willing their husbands safely back home.

Life whilst sweet was also precarious and exciting. Up there in the darkness, high in the star studded bowl of the sky, it was easy to recall that last trip down from the mess to the flights for that last briefing.

It had been a soft warm summer's day, England at its greenest, full of the smell of new mown hay, the leafy trees languid with the midday heat. Across the way some of the young wives were playing tennis, their sun tanned limbs accentuating the gleaming whiteness of their dresses, while before a huge chestnut tree, which served as a pavilion, a station cricket match was in progress.

This was England at its most leisurely. This was England

fiddling while Europe burned. It had seemed so incongruous that here were a few aircrew going off into the unknown while all around was peace and security. . .

Such reflections made me anxious to get the mission over so that in a few hours' time and after a brief sleep I could return to a more relaxed way of life. It was only now that I had time to realise that, as this trip had been highly secret and we had left for Abingdon in daylight, Dianne had not been there to wave me goodbye. . .

I found that thought faintly worrying and determinedly thrust it away. There was nothing to worry about. Dianne and I would soon be together again.

All was quiet in the plane. It was as though one was part of the entrails of a great bird as it was urging itself upwards, its wings trembling slightly, as it made its last supreme effort to gain the necessary height to take it across the last but tallest snowcapped peaks which barred its way back home. In the loneliness of my rear gun turret, my ears, encased in helmet and headphones, were always strained to catch any faint snatch of conversation between the crew up front huddled together in the nose of the plane. At times such as this when all the fear and excitement of the operation was over, the gunner in the isolation of the tail turret could feel lonely and vulnerable. It was cold too when flying above twelve thousand feet with no heating available. It was necessary to turn on the oxygen supply which at least produced an illusion of warmth and well-being.

The Air Ministry in 1940 was not entirely insensitive to the comfort of the reargunner, as it was realised that encased in a plastic bubble at a high altitude in winter, and surrounded by freezing metal controls, possible frost-bite was a serious problem. To counteract this, some clever boffin had thought up an ingenious answer. All rear turrets were supplied with two rubber hot water bottles just before take off. One was already hot and kept the airgunner's backside comfortably insulated from his cold metal seat for an hour or so. The other bottle contained a dry inert chemical and the only way to render it operative for the return journey was to urinate into it.

This was a most delicate and dangerous operation when one's loins were encased in a flying suit and the webbing of the parachute harness was strapped firmly between the legs. In the intense cold one split-second's over-exposure of the organ essential to start the desired chemical reaction would have more devastating effects than a touch of frost-bite on one's backside!

If airgunners were tortured by any fears, without doubt two were predominant. I personally had seen a gunner who had received terrible facial injuries from the cannon of a Messerschmitt which had crept up unnoticed. Another unfortunate had had his pelvis shattered and his loins destroyed. Against these two haunting hazards the young and virile aircrew gunners constantly invoked the protection of the Almighty.

As I sat there contemplating my good luck so far during this tour of Operations I thought I heard a short sharp crackle in my headphones but no voice came over the intercom. Then, with terrifying abruptness, the whole aircraft shuddered convulsively and took a violent uncontrolled lurch sideways. Into my headphones, hardly discernible, came the incredible order *'Abandon aircraft'!*

I couldn't believe it.

It couldn't be true.

I figured it must have been a figment of my imagination. I must have temporarily nodded off. It was a dream!

I had been closely confined in the turret for long hours which had been so much more uneventful than those earlier trips over Germany that it was entirely possible I could have nodded off.

But I knew - I just *knew* - that I hadn't.

I knew the drill backwards: the prescribed drill which all rear gunners had to learn until it was second nature if they were to survive. I had repeated it to myself *ad nauseam* during training and I clearly remembered a recent near catastrophe over Duisberg when bombing the docks on the Rhine. The plane had been picked up by searchlights, subjected to intense anti-aircraft fire, and had limped back home with thirty shrapnel holes scattered all over the fuselage. We'd all nearly had to jump then.

Now in this present emergency, crammed into the space of microseconds I could hear the instructor at the Gunnery School at Aldergrove in Northern Ireland coolly announcing in measured tones 'Should it be necessary to abandon aircraft the rear gunner will receive adequate warning. A magnesium flash bulb actuated by the pilot will light up the rear turret and the airgunner in response will press his received signal button, which will advise the pilot that evacuation procedures are in progress.

'The pilot' he droned on 'will then hold the plane straight and level to facilitate the crew to make their exit by parachute, after they have kicked out the emergency door amidships. The airgunner's turret is too confined to permit him to wear his parachute pack in position attached to his harness, which will consequently be stored in the fuselage near the emergency door.

'The rear gunner will immediately centralise his turret fore and aft, open the gun turret doors, scramble into the fuselage, snap his parachute pack on to his harness and make his exit.

'The pilot will be the last to leave'.

As a training crew, we had great fun practising the drill on the ground, and one bright spark asked the very tough, down to earth, Warrant Officer Instructor whether it would be possible to have a practice parachute jump to complete the emergency drill. 'Don't worry about that' came the laconic and cynical reply, 'your first jump will be your last'!

The order *'Abandon aircraft'* despite being hardly audible, had almost possessed the intensity of a scream, and I responded to it. In milliseconds I was extricating myself from the turret which fitted around me as closely as the cockpit of a racing car. I somersaulted backwards into the fuselage through the double swing doors as I had done to perfection so often in the emergency drills and was astounded to find that the emergency door had already been kicked out and I was only just in time to see three sinister grey figures leaping rapidly one after the other into the black void beyond without uttering a word or even casting a backward glance. This conjured up visions of convicts intent on a midnight escape, stealthily and quietly hoping to avoid detection. It was like a film - quite unreal!

At that moment the scene became even more dramatic - my blood ran cold as I realised that the fuselage was being lit by a fiery glow from within the cockpit from whence the crew had just fled. I realised that I had been left alone in a blazing plane with nobody at the controls! Obviously, there had been no time for the pilot to carry out the full emergency drill. A direct hit from an anti-aircraft shell had pierced the nose cone and set the cockpit alight. There had been no time for the pilot to sit it out calmly and, observing the correct procedures, hold the aircraft steady while the rest of the crew got out. It was a case of *'sauve qui peut'.* The training schedule had forgotten to cover such an eventuality!

Luckily I had received the message to abandon aircraft before the fire in the cockpit had completely destroyed the intercom system, or I would have bought it for sure, as had my friend Flying Officer Higson. He had been manning the gun in the front nose cone and had been killed instantly when the shell exploded, and his body was there, unbeknown to me, being consumed by those very flames by which I was now threatened.

Before I could clip on my parachute pack, the plane went into a steep nosedive with a slow spiral convulsion. What followed was like the worst part of a terrible nightmare. Still clutching the parachute pack I was pitched into a swirling vortex as if inside a barrel twisting, turning and falling over Niagara. Centrifugal force was pulling the parachute pack from my grasp and away from the clips chest high on my harness to which it had to be attached.

As I was hurled forward I kept a grim hold on the pack which was my lifeline. If I lost that, then I was lost too! I hit my head on the bulkhead door which, as I fell forward, mercifully closed and shielded me from the blazing cockpit.

It was a matter of seconds before the plane, having nosedived some thousand feet, had picked up enough speed for the nose to automatically lift like a paper dart, before it shuddered and juddered in its death throes, head up and tail down, to throw me spread-eagled back into the tail. And all this time a violent rush of air along the fuselage caused by the aircraft's plunging descent was attempting to suck me and everything else in the plane out through the gaping hole where the emergency door had originally been.

As I was catapulted backwards, the bulkhead door upfront swung open again, revealing the horrors of the blast furnace into which I feared I would be projected on the next headlong plunge.

It was as if some devil was manipulating the door, opening and closing it, and it was possible to see his mocking maniacal grin in the blazing inferno, first up, then down below, as the plane plummeted earthwards.

Down it dropped again, in its death agonies, forward again I was propelled never releasing my hold on the pack, pitting my whole strength against that demon force which pulled and tugged against me. Down dropped the bulkhead door with the precision of a stage managed scene. It was too precise to be real. It must be a nightmare. It was too horrific for the mind to contemplate, the fire, the buffeting, the helplessness, the demonic force tugging to prevent the parachute pack from being clipped to the harness, but the nightmare persisted. Three or four times the furnace door opened up, and my body was hurled towards the inferno to be halted at the last moment as the door swung shut and my head slammed against it. At any moment the plane must hit the ground!

Now terror really took hold.

By one last supreme effort I succeeded in clipping the parachute to one of the clips on the harness and that was enough. I took the next backward lurch of the aircraft and, somehow, I rode it. I got myself upright for long enough to fall sidelong through the hole in the wall of the plane and was greedily sucked into the howling slipstream as the plane continued its death dive.

Frantically, with my left hand, I grabbed for the parachute's rip cord but I couldn't find it. It was not where I instinctively knew it should be had the parachute been attached to both its clips. With the speed of lightning I scrabbled for it with my other hand and suddenly found it. I pulled it in frenzied fury.

Instantly, there was a sound overhead like the noise of a torn sail flapping furiously in a gale and my descent was arrested by a jerk so sudden and violent that I vomited involuntarily. At that intense moment of relief, attached by only one clip to my parachute, I saw the plane as a mass of flames plunging by, almost colliding with me and taking me with it, before it exploded below in a ball of fire and a fountain of sparks.

In the same instant, I realised that I was falling too quickly. My chute wasn't functioning properly. With horror, I guessed what had happened.

Because it had not been properly clipped to the harness, the parachute had failed to open completely and the guidelines had become hopelessly entangled. I now knew my chute was only partially open and I was almost in free fall.

And I was heading straight for the blazing aircraft below.

3

Captured

I HIT THE GROUND WITH SUCH FORCE that I was instantly knocked unconscious.

I lay there completely oblivious to everything except for brief occasions when consciousness fitfully returned. In those short, hardly lucid, moments I was aware of the voluminous canopy of the parachute enveloping me and, in my confused state, thought I was back in Trinidad under my mosquito net, safe and sound in bed! I was conscious of a buzzing in my ears and this my bemused mind convinced me was made by a horde of mosquitoes trying to get inside the net. I made half hearted attempts to pull it more securely over the bed as I blacked out again.

When I recovered sufficiently to realise what had really happened, it was broad daylight and the sun was well up in a cloudless August sky. I tried to sit up, but the pain in my back wouldn't let me. It was so intense. My spine felt as though it had been shattered into a thousand pieces all grating and grinding together. My sight too was badly blurred. I found it difficult to focus, and was aware of a lump of quite alarming proportions at the base of my skull. Never had I felt so helpless, so deserted, so alone and so exposed.

I had landed in a field of maize some five feet tall high

above which stretched a series of high tension power cables. I was lying at the foot of a tall metal pylon on which was a large red and black sign bearing a skull and crossbones, a ghoulish reminder of what my fate would have been if my chute had become entangled with the power lines. Luckily, in spite of it all, I was still alive. How badly injured I did not know, but my first instinct was for survival, to keep concealed and keep my wits about me.

Suddenly I was startled to hear the sound of a gunshot a few fields away, which made me realise people were in the close vicinity.

I made a desperate effort while still on my back to pull my parachute together into a heap well below the top of the maize so it wouldn't easily be seen. With this painfully achieved, I crawled very slowly towards the edge of the field and dropped down into a deep bramble-covered ditch which completely concealed me.

Lying there, I calmly assessed my position. I was now a fugitive in enemy territory, which gave me a very naked feeling. I had no friends nearby to call on for aid and support. I was on my own.

It would have been some consolation if there'd been some way of letting my comrades know as they'd winged their way home that I was still alive. They would certainly have seen our plane go down in flames and witnessed its explosive disintegration on impact. What would they have thought? If they hadn't seen the chutes, only one thing. I had seen many friends meet their fate over German targets in that selfsame way.

Even if the chutes had been spotted, and counted, they

would have added up to one short. And so, at best, the whole crew would be posted 'Missing over enemy territory' until more positive information emerged. At worst, we could all be presumed dead.

I thought of Dianne and of her shock when "C" for Charlie failed to return to Leeming. But at least she had been spared a last formal goodbye on the runway. It was as though fate had been kind for once, knowing what was in store, and I vividly remembered our particularly warm and loving embrace when, in private, we had lingeringly kissed our last fond farewell.

I was wearing a Mae West inflatable jacket and parachute harness over flying overalls, sheepskin leather flying jacket and knee-high fleece-lined leather flying boots. Beneath all of this was my RAF officer's uniform. My flying helmet had blown away as I had jumped from the plane. The sound of that gunshot was echoing in my brain. It worried me.

The Italian farmer would by now most probably have discovered the parachute hidden in the middle of his field, which would present him with a problem of conscience. It would be tempting to secrete the yards and yards of fine silk which could be made into garments which would fetch a fortune on the black market. Against this temptation he would have to weigh his patriotic feelings and perhaps hand over his booty to the military authorities who would have put guards on the downed plane. At first light, the burned out wreckage of the plane would have been inspected and the charred remains of one crew member found, leading the authorities to the assumption that they had all the other occupants of the plane to round up. They'd be looking for us and if the farmer had handed over my chute they would know where to start.

With these thoughts running through my mind as I lay on my dry but uncomfortable bed of brambles and nettles, fatigue overtook me and I fell into an uneasy fitful sleep, surfacing unwillingly every now and again when dragged back to consciousness by the increasing pain in my back and neck. At times when I had managed to arouse myself sufficiently I raised my head carefully to look around me.

The field was bordered by a main road along which heavy traffic moved incessantly. I calculated that I had been about twenty-four hours without food. Luckily, I had in my pocket the emergency iron rations carried by all aircrew to meet this situation, and so I was able to gnaw at the extra-thick, extra-hard bar of enriched bitter chocolate, and quenched my thirst with the juicy blackberries growing everywhere in profusion.

It was while still lying flat on my back to pick the blackberries above my head that I realised that something serious had happened to my sight. I had double vision Whatever I focused on appeared twice over, so to get a proper view of what I was looking at I had to put my hand over one eye and then peer out through the other. I realised that this disorientation must be connected with the large bump at the base of my skull. I explored it tentatively with my fingers, even licking them first to detect any dried blood, but the skin seemed unbroken.

Soon the sun began to fall noticeably from its zenith. In a few more hours twilight would descend and then night would overtake these daylight hours of suspense. I realised that my best hope of escaping detection was to remove myself from the search area, as more and more troops and police were likely to be drafted in as the search was intensified. I calculated that it must now be around five o'clock in the afternoon as traffic on the road increased visibly, and hordes of men appeared on bicycles, presumably on their way home from work in some nearby town. Conceivably this could have been the town we had just bombed - Turin. I felt I would get little sympathy from them if they discovered my hideout. I had to get away. There were two options I could consider for escape purposes, either to make for Switzerland or Southern (unoccupied) France.

Switzerland seemed the most appealing. Aircrew were regularly briefed on escape routes if shot down, and Allied airmen had been known to have been helped back to England, but just how this had been achieved was never discussed. To get to Switzerland from Germany was easy compared to getting over the border from Italy which meant surmounting the Alpine barrier, unthinkable in my condition. The Alps had proved a problem to Hannibal centuries ago although his troops were fit and had elephants to help them. Switzerland was definitely out. So it was to be France then, which I calculated lay due west. If I kept a little south of west it might be easy to cross the Italian border somewhere along the coast.

With an effort I heaved myself up and took stock of my appearance, trying to decide how I could camouflage my RAF clothes to look more like a civilian. I stripped myself of all trappings to do with flying and stamped them well down amongst the brambles, leaving me standing in my tunic. It then took only a few moments to effect an acceptable transformation. The blue-grey serge trousers were pulled down over the tops of the flying boots to conceal them and the rollneck grey sweater would pass as civilian gear, so all that was left was to take off the tunic, turn it inside out to hide the telltale wings, buttons and braid and to carry it over my arm. If only I had been physically fit I would have warmed to the challenge and felt quite elated at my chances of making good my escape.

I ambled as casually as possible on to the road from the edge of the field as though I had been working there, and was now homeward bound. If only I'd a bicycle I felt I could get clean away and not be as conspicuous as I was on foot, particularly as my back was giving me trouble and I was not walking well.

Keeping on the grass verge, I went westwards towards the setting sun. Cars were hurtling along the highway, the cyclists so preoccupied with avoiding each other and the other traffic, that nobody cast even so much as a glance at the poor peasant lad wending his way home after a hard days work in the fields!

The road ran through very sparsely inhabited country. There were few houses. Signposts pointed off down side roads to villages along the way, but the village names meant nothing to me and gave me no clue as to my whereabouts. The longer I walked, apparently exciting no curiosity whatsoever, the more my expectations rose. Nobody appeared interested in me or suspicious of me and why should they? Men in northern Italy were often tall and fair, quite different from their swarthy neighbours in the south, and my face unshaven for twenty-four hours gave me an even more workmanlike country appearance.

I walked on and on westward, deafened by the strident hoots from car horns as drivers appeared to grow ever more impatient as it got darker. I now began to question whether I would look more conspicuous walking along the road in the dark than I would in daylight. One was likely to be noticed and watched more closely when picked out by the lights of passing cars, but it was a happy thought that the further I walked the further I was getting away from the prime search area.

Just as I contemplated the attraction of hiding up for the night and taking much needed rest from my back pain, I suddenly sensed that above the usual cacophony of blaring car horns there was a much more strident wailing noise closing up quickly behind me. I dared not look back as I realised that the approaching vehicle was slowing sharply as it approached me, and I was picked out by a powerful searchlight which projected my silhouette sharply ahead. It would be fatal to betray any panic. I could only hope that I was not the object of anything more than curiosity and, clothed as I was, I could not be one of the missing airmen they were so obviously seeking.

The car shot past me and for a moment I believed my prayers had been answered, but then with a violent screeching of brakes the car jerked to a halt and a couple of uniformed armed policemen rushed towards me, gesticulating and shouting. There was no preamble. There were no polite questions. In a fascist state at war it was act first and talk later. They were going to show few of the proprieties to any suspect. In seconds the back doors of the van were opened and I was unceremoniously bundled inside on to a mattress. The doors were slammed shut and locked with a shattering finality and the car sped off into the night, its siren blaring with even more gusto. I sprawled there in the dark wondering what would happen to me next, but this period of uncertainty was short lived when the van jerked to a halt again, the doors were pulled open, and I was bundled roughly ahead of the policemen into their local police station.

It was frugally furnished. A single large portrait of Mussolini in a dramatic pose filled one wall, while plastered everywhere were pictures of assorted criminals not unlike the 'Wanted' posters in Hollywood westerns. The police officers were in a great state of excitement. Everybody was shouting at everybody else, telephones were ringing and nobody was composed enough to answer them. My arrival had obviously caused as much commotion as if Il Duce himself had unexpectedly arrived on the scene. I didn't understand one word of what anyone was saying. All I could do was slouch on an uncomfortable chair with one hand pressed into the small of my back to try help relieve the pain. The other hand I held up over one eye so that I could focus the other on the charade now being enacted. It gradually became apparent to my captors that their prisoner was suffering from some injuries but without an interpreter it was impossible to establish any meaningful rapport.

They naturally soon discovered that my tunic had been turned inside out, and the sight of my braid and my badges made them more unintelligibly voluble than ever.

After a while a young fair-haired English girl, of about eighteen years of age, was ushered in to interpret. She told me she had been governess to a wealthy Italian family in the neighbourhood before the outbreak of war and I supposed she was possibly now in some kind of internment. But I also noted that she had been escorted into the room by a young debonair carabiniere officer who, from the way he was behaving towards her, obviously knew quite a good deal about her less obvious accomplishments.

Under the direction of an aggressive, heavily bemedalled officer, the girl interpreted in her cultured governess voice what my inquisitors volubly demanded; name, rank, service number, operational station in England, target in Italy, number of planes on the raid etc. Apart from the first three - name, rank and number - these were all questions which aircrew were forbidden to answer in the event of being taken prisoner. Name, rank and service number was the only information a prisoner was required to give to an enemy under the terms of the Geneva Convention to which Great Britain and Italy were both signatories and which both were obliged to observe. Furnishing an enemy with more information than this could, we knew well, be detrimental to the security of our country.

After lengthy cajoling and showing signs of increased frustration at not being able to extract more than name, rank and number from me, the young interpreter took rapid instruction in a feverish aside with the senior officer. She came back to advise me in a contrived dramatic whisper that as I had given them no information to connect me with the plane which had been shot down, and as I was not wearing flying kit, my silence could be treated very seriously indeed. Clearly, she said, since I had disguised myself as a civilian I was laying myself open to being shot as a spy. This was obviously calculated to bring a recalcitrant prisoner to heel and to encourage more co-operation.

I did not oblige.

By this time I was utterly exhausted and enquired whether I could be given some medical assistance as the pain in my spine and back of my head was getting worse and, in fact, being shot as a spy was an option I would have gladly considered. My appeal was met with the selfsame stubborn intransigence with which I was stonewalling their questions. The interrogation continued unabated.

Then the emphasis suddenly switched from questions about England to where I had dumped my flying gear if I truly was one of the airmen they were seeking? I could only reply that it was hidden in a field of maize crossed by overhead power cables supported on pylons. My gear was in a ditch which bordered the field. Beyond was the highway. It was not possible to be much more precise. They too were becoming exhausted with the questioning and seized this as a convenient moment to break off.

I was driven away in a car seated between two officers and conducted on a countrywide tour in the moonlight. Many blanks were drawn before they hit upon the correct location, recognised by the self-identifying pylons crossing a large field of maize.

In seconds the two other police officers in the front of the car had leapt out and were ploughing through the high corn, each bent on outdoing the other to be first to discover any telltale clues. From the large area of flattened corn they soon found, it would have been clear to them that my story had substance but my parachute was nowhere to be seen. The hoped for prize had eluded them. No doubt the farmer had been there first - but whether he received a citizen's medal for discovering the parachute, or an exemplary sentence for concealing vital information in wartime, I never knew.

It was then easy to follow my tracks through the trodden down corn to the ditch at the edge of the field, where they retrieved sufficient flying gear to clear me of the charge of being a spy.

Italy had been at war only about ten weeks so it was easy to understand their excitement at having a captured RAF officer in their possession in that little village and it was not long before I was back in the police station under more interrogation. The telephones jangled even more frequently and, as officers rushed here and there to answer them, it was obvious from their respectful demeanour that they were talking to those in higher authority who were no doubt critical of the progress that the local interrogations had made. It was probably this lack of progress which led to my being bundled off again with a military escort who paid no heed to my pleas for a drink of water and medical assistance.

After a long and furious journey across country we slowed down to a more sedate pace as we entered the well lit streets of a thriving metropolis which I calculated would be Turin. We halted before a large building which I took to be the area military headquarters and I was ushered inside with some considerable respect by the officers and not a little trepidation on my part. Here in more impressive surroundings the questioning began again, this time conducted by high ranking military personnel accompanied by gentlemen in civilian clothes whom I surmised were Germans incognito, long versed in the art of interrogation of prisoners of war.

In front of the assembled inquisition stood a stark, straight backed and uncomfortable looking chair, which contrasted sharply with the exaggerated luxury of those occupied by my interrogators. Focused on to the solitary chair was a light of almost blinding intensity in the otherwise dimly lit room. The lighting gave the effect of a dramatic stage setting and I was pushed deftly into its centre, exhausted, hungry, thirsty and in considerable pain. I had now been without food for nearly forty-eight hours. No pleas for assistance of any kind were heeded, as they prepared for the clinically sophisticated interrogation to be directed by experts in the art of breaking down a prisoner's resistance.

I was ready for the worst.

I reversed the chair and sat astride it, my body sagging forward against its high back as I faced my inquisitors. My eyes, now quite painful and unable to focus in unison, were equally unable to cope with the blinding light which blazed down upon me so I allowed my head to roll forward. In this slumped position I found a little comfort as the chair back took some of the weight off my injured spine.

The proceedings opened with a hint of nicely calculated encouragement when I was offered a cigarette while the interrogators lit up their own. I did not even give them the courtesy of looking up, smoking had not been any more to me than a social grace to be enjoyed in convivial company and I sensed this was not to be a convivial occasion.

The questioning began in conciliatory tones, which my interrogators considered might be more productive, but their attitude quickly changed when they realised that no amount of cajoling would be of use against a person who refused to answer their questions and did nothing except plead for a few hours sleep. I was assured that they were conscious of my injuries and knew how tired I must be. They were civilised people. Naturally, hospital treatment had been laid on for me. But a few small, insignificant details must be provided by me first.

And the details they wanted really were very small and insignificant, they repeated, for they already knew a great deal about me. The fact that I was from No. 10 Squadron, for instance and that my plane had crossed the English coast over Hastings. They had the names of the surviving crew and confirmed my fears that the co-pilot Flying Officer Higson had perished.

Now all they required from me were a few moments of co-operation and I could then receive all the refreshment and medical attention I needed. Although on the verge of collapse my mind remained increasingly alert. I realised that the information they had revealed need not have been extorted from the other survivors whom they obviously had in custody, since their names had been given to me correctly. The German tracking stations along the French coast could have registered an incursion into their airspace via Hastings. All they needed was confirmation.

They would have been able to ascertain from the burnt out wreck that the plane was a Whitley bomber. They knew that Whitleys were operated by bomber squadrons in Yorkshire and Lincolnshire and they made it abundantly clear they wanted to know the exact location. To me, such meagre information might hardly seem worth the effort they were prepared to exert, but it was obviously very important to them.

The night had ticked by in a fruitless exertion. I calculated in my bemused state that it must now be August 17th when, with a feverish flurry of papers and a babble of tongues from the bench, the proceedings broke up. My interrogators had obviously concluded they were just as much in need of sleep as was their prisoner.

At long last I could expect some relief. I was taken to a small clinic within the building in which were two iron beds and offered a drink of water which, on account of my advanced stage of exhaustion, was less important than before. All I needed was sleep!

I had collapsed fully clothed on the bed when a hospital orderly appeared with some food in a shallow enamelled bowl: the most brilliant green peas surmounted by the yellowest of yellow fried egg. It all looked so unreal in the bright lights of the clinic that I questioned whether it was not a figment of my imagination, but I did not have the time to put it to the test. The bowl was removed as abruptly as it had appeared, and left me reflecting whether this was not another refinement of the interrogation process which I hoped had come to an end. As the bowl went out through the door two guards came in and I was escorted off to a basement room with a bare stone flagged floor.

A grey blanketed bed beckoned me in one corner. I threw myself on to it despite my disabilities and as the iron door closed with an earsplitting clang I was asleep.

It was a fitful sleep, for as soon as the initial fatigue wore off I was in considerable pain, but I pulled myself up off the bed to survey my surroundings through a very small iron-grilled window. The view was non-existent and as I cast my blinkered eye over the iron door, stone walls and floor, I reflected that this would be all I could expect of a prisoner-of-war camp for the duration.

After a few hours of despondency my spirits were revived by the appearance of some warm sweet coffee and a bread roll. I assumed that the production of the long promised food signalled that the interrogation had really been called off and I was not going to allow the food to disappear as had the previous brief offering. I was ravenous!

That evening I was on the move again. Thankfully the rudimentary accommodation was not to be my fixed abode as I had feared. I was now to be accommodated at an army camp some way outside Turin and most of the night I was subjected to visits from officers who were very curious to see what a captured RAF officer looked like.

The next morning the Colonel in charge of the barracks called at the Guard Room and ordered me to accompany him and two armed guards on his rounds of the camp. He was obviously eccentric as he also brought along a black bear on a chain. I am sure that my haggard and unkempt appearance only added to this bizarre circus. The colonel could speak no English but through an interpreter he told me I was to be allowed to attend the funeral of my colleague Flying Officer Higson, whose charred remains had been recovered from the burnt out plane.

The funeral was in the little village of Ceresola d'Alba and as I got out of the Colonel's car next morning, I was very relieved to see standing near the churchyard gate Sgts. Green, Millington and Davis, surrounded by a posse of armed guards. We were kept apart and I was forbidden to speak to them as the four of us bore our gallant comrade shoulder high in a very small coffin, but they could not prevent me from satisfying myself that they had kept their nerve and secrets during their first few days of traumatic captivity.

The funeral was simple. As the coffin was lowered into the grave a guard of honour fired a volley overhead, while several kind-hearted women stepped forward to place little bunches of flowers on the grave for which we could only make a small nod of grateful acknowledgement which did not go unnoticed. It was a touching gesture of those village mothers, some of whom may well have known what it was to lose a soldier son in war in a distant country like Abyssinia or Spain, as far away from home as was our friend now laid to rest.

Next morning, after another night at the army camp, I was put on a train in a first class compartment with an armed guard on either side of me and two more stationed in the corridor outside the compartment to deter over-inquisitive passengers. The blinds in the compartment were drawn so I was not able to catch even a glimpse of the country through which we were passing.

After many hours the train pulled into Rome where I was met by a body of troops and cars worthy of the visit of someone of much greater importance. We sped through the streets of the city to the headquarters of the Italian Air Force, the *Reggia Aeronautica,* where I spent a very exhausting day being interviewed by all the top people, who appeared more intent on actually seeing a real live captured RAF officer than becoming involved in the wearisome business of digging out small scraps of information for intelligence purposes.

I was then subjected to a lengthy and exhaustive medical examination similar to that undergone by cadets at home

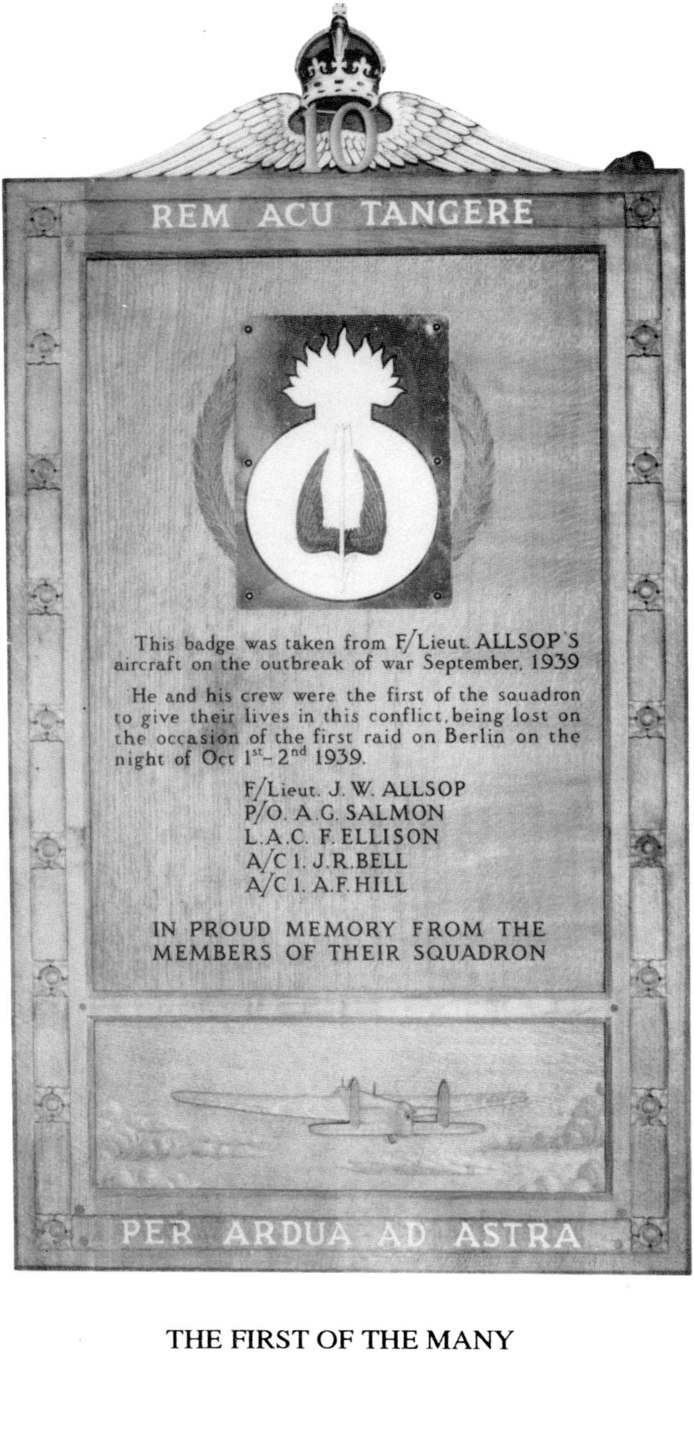

THE FIRST OF THE MANY

RAF ALDERGROVE, NORTHERN IRELAND
AIR GUNNERS' COURSE
January - February 1940

(Front Row, left to right) Pilot Officers
Watt, Oliver, Johnson, Lovett, Green, Mailer, Lane,
Drake-Carnell, Whigham

FUNERAL OF F/O HIGSON AT CERESOLA D'ALBA
August 1940

The Author is the rear pall-bearer

THE GRAVE OF F/O HIGSON AT CERESOLA D'ALBA

THE WHITLEY BOMBER REAR TURRET
OCCUPIED BY THE AUTHOR

No. 10 Squadron, RAF Dishforth and RAF Leeming, 1940

before being granted a commission. When I pointed out the damage to my back and my head I was told there was nothing to be done about it and I must realise time was a great healer! I quickly reached the conclusion that the real purpose of the medical examination was to compare the standards of fitness of their own Service with that of RAF officers and that consequently my own personal problems were no concern of theirs.

The examination over, I was transferred to an Officers' Mess at the air base at Centocelli Rome where my 'cell' was a bedroom in one wing which was closely guarded day and night.

Here, for the first time, I was treated like an officer and a gentleman. I enjoyed this luxury. The food was good and most evenings, demonstrating the comradeship of the air, I would be visited by Italian pilots who would bring cigarettes and drinks to share with me. Although I appreciated their company, I was very much on my guard as I was conscious that amongst the friendly, well-meaning visitors there could have been an intelligence man, masquerading as a pilot, anxious to get information that more austere treatment had denied them.

After two weeks I was advised that the Italians had completed a permanent prisoner-of-war camp to which I was to be transferred. The Camp was at Sulmona and the Italian Colonel entrusted to deliver me there was most relieved when he was able to hand me over safe and sound to the Camp Commandant.

4

Sulmona

THE PRISONER OF WAR CAMP AT SULMONA was the first to be built by the Italians, and was completed some two months after they had entered the war. A conglomeration of roughly built brick huts, its official name was *Fonte de Latte* - Fountain of Milk - but just why it should have been so named even the most cynical of Italians, even allowing for their innate romanticism, could never explain. The milk of human kindness was certainly not the liquid in question.

It was surrounded by concrete walls about eighteen feet high, on top of which was a barbed wire entanglement. Security was reinforced with a series of sentry boxes beyond the walls between which armed soldiers patrolled night and day, assisted during the hours of darkness by brilliant arc lights spaced out along the top of the walls every few yards and backed up with powerful swivelling searchlights. It was deemed escape-proof. To me was afforded the doubtful privilege of being the first inmate, others arriving later that day. I found it very basic and spartan after my recent stay in the Air Force Officers' Mess in Rome.

Flight Lieutenant Gregory who turned up later was a South African by birth who had joined the RAF before the war and had been shot down flying a reconnaissance operation from

Malta. He was quite an extrovert character and was to be a close companion in the uncharted years which lay ahead. One needed friendship when surrounded by hostile circumstances, and it was interesting to see how swiftly incoming prisoners formed alliances which grew into close friendships as time passed and more and more prisoners arrived. And these were friendships based not so much on whether one was RAF, Army or Navy but on something much more subtle and intangible.

Most of these deep friendships endured the test of time, and ensured that the individual survived as a member of a group in the starkly competitive and ruthless existence of a prison camp much more easily than one would on one's own.

The camp at Sulmona was for officers only. In fact it was doubtful whether Italy, which had been part of the Axis war machine for such a short time, had many other-rank PoWs as the country had so far been only the target of a few special operations involving highly trained men, who were usually commissioned officers. For the Italians, surveying their catch, it was a question of quality not quantity. The thousands of soldiers yet to be captured in North Africa by Rommel and his elite German Afrika Corps and dumped on the Italians for safe keeping had not yet arrived.

In a few days the camp's complement was increased by a Lieutenant Commander and three Lieutenants from a British submarine, rather ignominiously captured when an Italian destroyer came unexpectedly upon their craft on a moonlit night, placidly sitting on the surface recharging its batteries after being harried all day by the enemy who had reason to suspect its presence near Taranto. A salvo of shells from the

Italian destroyer had rapidly prevented her from diving to safety. Much to their chagrin, we made a point of frequently questioning our naval friends, as to whether they were all asleep at the time, as the exposure of their submarine on the surface should have required more than usual vigilance.

A more heroic group of mariners quickly followed them into the camp, a batch of Fleet Air Arm men operating Swordfish aircraft from the aircraft carrier *Illustrious.* Twenty one 'stringbags' had been assigned to the very bold and dangerous operation of attacking the Italian fleet which was holed up in Taranto harbour. Aerial torpedoes were dropped from as low as thirty feet, the planes having to contend with murderous fire from anti-aircraft batteries and steel nets held in position over the harbour by barrage balloons.

This operation had called for the greatest precision and considerable courage, so the planes had to be flown by pilots of great experience, in this case Lieutenant Commanders aided by skilled lieutenants expert in navigation. Many of the Italian warships were damaged severely by the Swordfish attack. In fact, the aircraft inflicted more damage on the enemy than the Grand Fleet had inflicted on the Germans at Jutland.

Lt. Commander (later Captain) Williamson, one of many unsung heroes of the war, scored a direct hit on the battleship *Conte de Cavour*, but was shot down and spent the rest of the war as a PoW. We did not know in Sulmona he was to receive the D.S.O. for his part in the operation. The Naval Historian later suggested that his reward should really have been the V.C.

The ranks of Fleet Air Arm officers were soon swelled by

a number of senior naval lieutenants who had their war potential recklessly squandered before they'd had time to be effective against the enemy. These pilots were operating planes from the carrier *Ark Royal.* When the carrier was considered to be near enough to Malta for the planes to make the rest of the journey under their own power, rather than risk the Ark sailing too deeply into hostile waters, the planes took off, only to run out of fuel before making landfall.

Someone had grossly miscalculated.

The planes, which were desperately needed for the defence of Malta, had to ditch in the sea. Some pilots were lucky to be picked up by Italian destroyers patrolling the area. One pilot was adrift with his two crew members for ten days and was washed up on the North African coast, but not before his companions had died from exposure. The pilot was found by Arabs on the beach unconscious with his swollen tongue protruding grotesquely from between his swollen and salt burned lips. He was tended by the Arabs in a desert camp near Benghazi, but only for just as long as it took to revive him sufficiently to be turned over to the Italian troops in the neighbourhood for some petty reward.

Another early intake was a contingent of Commandos who, led by a Major (Welsh Guards), had been dropped by parachute in the middle of Italy to blow up a vital viaduct. Their mission was 100% successful but they were prevented from making a rendezvous with the submarine which was to pick them up. They were all rounded up but not before a young Canadian lieutenant, who shall remain nameless, had killed several of the Italian soldiers in the process.

Why the Italians had taken him alive we could never

understand, and he would often regale us with blood-thirsty stories of how he had slit their throats in fierce hand to hand fighting, as at that time he had still believed that if, somehow, he overcame the opposition he would keep the rendezvous with the submarine.

Although we got to know him intimately in the camp, he always remained a sinister character, a loner of course, but also certainly a brave commando who had unquestioningly carried out his orders as he was expected to, with little regard for his own safety.

It must surely have been obvious to the camp's Italian commandant that it would be hard to keep virile, young officers quiet for long within the confines of high walls and barbed wire entanglements. When it was first occupied, some of the camp's spartan accommodation blocks were having a few finishing touches applied by a team of Italian workmen under the watchful eyes of a posse of soldiers. They weren't there to discipline the workforce but to keep it and the *kriegies,* the PoWs well apart.

It was not that the work*men* were an attraction, except that we could admire their skill and watching someone else work has always been a great British hobby. Besides, in the camp it relieved the boredom to some extent. But the principal draw was the builders' female assistant - a teenager whose features were as beautiful as her lithe, young figure.

In an all male prisoner-of-war camp the appearance of *any* woman was certain to attract interest. And when that woman was both young and beautiful that interest was redoubled. Her job was to mix the cement, a task more suited to a strong young male, but such was Mussolini's obsession with getting all Italian males into uniform, that women were being conscripted into hard construction work as well as being put into factories.

It was the kriegies' daily pre-occupation to get as close to the girl as the guardian soldiers would allow and to embarrass her with such light hearted banter as they could manage with their limited knowledge of the language. The girl was a star attraction for weeks, fêted by the prisoners not only on her own account but also because the guards seemed to enjoy the banter and, consequently didn't keep a close watch on the builders' small tools, which consequently had a habit of disappearing.

Later, many of these proved to be very useful in escape attempts.

For already such plans were being eagerly discussed. Back in England it had been impressed upon all of us that, if captured by the enemy, our first duty was to try to escape. It was realised that most escapes were doomed to failure, but every attempt kept an increasing number of the enemy's troops tied up in security duties, when they could have been better deployed on active service.

Sulmona, we realised, was not far from Italy's east coast and it would not be impossible for escaped prisoners, particularly the naval officers, to cross over to the Greek islands if an unsuspecting fisherman's boat could be stolen at night. The contemplation of such escapades was exciting and wetted one's appetite for action. In the days that followed an Escape Committee was formed and plans to dig a tunnel were discussed in elaborate detail.

To the uninitiated, the preliminaries to digging a tunnel

must be explained. To reduce its length, the labour needed and the time required for completion, the tunnel had to run from a building near to a perimeter wall. Access to the tunnel would be through a trapdoor which would have to be ingeniously hidden. In the particular building finally selected for our first shaft, there was a wood-burning stove standing on tiles and, with a little persuasion, this could be moved sideways. The tiles on which it stood were then lifted and cemented on to a wooden square (all materials 'borrowed' from the Italian builders) and a corresponding square of the earth floor scraped away to receive the tiles back again.

This tiled wooden square now formed the cover, the trapdoor, of our intended tunnel and beneath it we started sinking the main shaft.

With the tiles back in place and the stove restored to its original position everything looked normal and would arouse no suspicion. Yet, below the tiles, a shaft about ten feet deep and three feet wide was rapidly hollowed out.

In this cramped space, a digger could labour away with whatever suitable tools we had managed to acquire - nothing more, in this case, than a small iron bar. At a depth of ten to twelve feet the soil was fairly well compacted and it was then possible to start the main tunnel from the bottom of the shaft with a minimum of timbering to shore up the roof to prevent it caving in.

The tunnel was dug high enough and wide enough to allow the beefiest one of us to wriggle through. At first two people at a time were employed in the tunnel, one to dig, the other to claw back the dislodged earth, which was extremely hard work in such a restricted space.

Light had to be provided for the work underground and this came from a lamp made out of a small bottle of olive oil with a wick of string. As the digger worked on the earth wall ahead with the lamp in front of him he used up the small amount of air which could enter the tunnel around his body. Consequently, the lamp, deprived of oxygen, was constantly going out. To get more air along the tunnel as it progressed a cardboard and paper pump was fashioned, which could push air through a narrow cloth pipe to the workers. This posed another problem. The cloth pipe had to be kept constantly wet to keep the air from escaping, so the digger and his mate had to urinate over it regularly to keep it moist. This was certainly the most convenient way to get water down to where it was needed but it did little to clear the foetid atmosphere of the workplace, and the tunnellers' thirst was prodigious.

After the work had advanced laboriously for several yards it came up against the face of a large wall of rock which could only be dealt with by digging out another six foot deep shaft to take the tunnel under the obstacle and on again in the right direction. This greatly increased problems with the air supply and made getting to and from the workface more difficult, as well as adding to the burden of extracting the dislodged earth.

It was not possible to turn in the tunnel, and the only way to traverse it was to wriggle to the rock face and then take a nosedive down to the bottom of the second shaft. At times the air at the workface seemed non-existent and it was necessary for both tunnellers to wriggle back into the first shaft for a breather.

Workers were replaced every half an hour, so exhausting were the conditions, and it was not surprising that, at times it was difficult to find more volunteers willing to assist.

On occasion, helpers fell prey to acute claustrophobia and reluctantly had to cry off, particularly following subsidences which, though minor, created a lot of alarm in such cramped conditions.

In spite of all the hazards just working on the tunnel gave everyone involved a tremendous lift. We all felt that in a very positive way we were doing what we could to break free of this place and hit back at the enemy. Nevertheless, we were well aware of the risks we ran and were only too ready to sympathise with those who could not carry on any further.

Throughout, it was necessary to have a sophisticated system of security operating above ground so that the tunnel opening was only exposed momentarily to allow ingress and egress, before the trapdoor was lowered and the stove swung back again into position. The men entrusted with opening and closing the tunnel were highly skilled and practised in the operation, so it took only a matter of seconds, reminiscent of the highly skilled pit mechanics in motor racing who are drilled to change tyres and fill up petrol tanks with lightning precision.

While digging was in progress teams of watchers kept the main gate under constant surveillance and the entry of any Italian was swiftly signalled to those at the tunnel entrance. A series of loud taps in code on the trapdoor told the workers below to suspend operations immediately.

Interrupted by delays caused by surprise inspections as well as the scheduled roll calls, work proceeded slowly day by day, week by week until excitement began to mount when it was realised that, provided the tunnel was truly on course, its length meant that we had gone under the perimeter wall and we were now tunnelling beyond the confines of the prison. All we needed was a final spurt, another dozen yards or so and breakout was possible.

But our excitement was short-lived, for at that precise moment when success was almost within our grasp disaster struck. As the length of the tunnel had grown it had become ever more difficult to find sufficient material to shore up the roof. Now, as the end was clearly in sight, it was decided to press on without timbering and take the risk, rather than hold up the operation whilst more was laboriously 'borrowed'. And this was when the inevitable happened.

There was a sudden subsidence. It had happened often before, nothing that could not be cleared, but this one occurred between the digger at the workface and his mate behind him. The more the digger's mate strove to scoop the loose earth away, the faster it fell, whilst its weight flattened the airtube and left the digger at the workface totally in the dark without sufficient air to breath.

There was nothing to be done but to abandon all our cherished hopes of escape and turn to the desperate and immediate task of getting the entombed digger out of the tunnel. An urgent message was at once sent to the Italian Commandant and in no time at all the camp was filled with troops and digging equipment. After what seemed an eternity the position of the trapped man was plotted just inside the camp perimeter wall and amid a flurry and frantic digging and frenzied instructions - *'Piano! Piano! Basta! Basta!'* - the tunnel end was revealed and a very confused, filthy, half suffocated, almost naked man was pulled out legs first, like a rabbit from its burrow by an excited poacher, to relieved whoops of joy from the anxious prisoners.

Lengthy inquests were held by the Italian authorities. Top Brass came from Rome. They were not surprised that a tunnel had been dug, tunnels have had their place in the history of prison camps for centuries, but they were by no means convinced that a tunnel so long and elaborate could have been dug with only the aid of one small iron bar and much time was spent turning the camp upside down in an effort to find more sophisticated tools.

The rescued digger was the only individual who could be positively connected with the tunnel and he was conveyed to the cooler for thirty days solitary confinement. At the same time, all privileges were withdrawn from all the other prisoners for the same period.

This meant that weekly walks supervised by the Italian officers and policed by armed guards were stopped for a time, but gradually most things returned to normal. The one thing that didn't ease was camp security. This was tightened up, so random spot checks were more frequent and surveillance was much more intensive.

It was evident that escape attempts were going to be even more difficult and hazardous operations in the future.

5

The Second Escape Attempt

IT WAS A RED LETTER DAY when, after about three months, the supervised walks with armed patrols were resumed, probably as a result of complaints made to visiting Red Cross officials from Geneva that some camp privileges had not been reinstated.

The real reason the Italians were displeased with us was that in these early days of the war they still thought of us as officers and English gentlemen and had been genuinely upset when, as they saw it, their trust in the 'English gentlemen' had been betrayed.

The next escape effort had to be less elaborate than the first and as I had taken an active part in the tunnel-digging up to the very end, the Senior British Officer through whom all escape plans had to be co-ordinated, was agreeable to our next plan when I put it to him. It did not however find universal acceptance among all of the kriegies. Those who were keen to preserve gentlemanly privileges and make life a little easier in the camp were naturally not in favour. The plan was for just four of us to escape during one of the organised walks. To have included more than four would have been impossible. The escape required precision timing and swift action, so careful planning was vital.

Once a week we were taken in groups about thirty-five strong for a walk in the country, accompanied by several Italian officers from the administration staff and guarded on each side by a file of ten soldiers, with one leading and another bringing up the rear. The officers carried pistols, the soldiers were armed with rifles and bayonets.

There was only one dusty track of a road out of the camp, and this led through a small village about a mile away, so we took this route regularly and always attracted a lot of interest from the villagers. We were a cheery motley crowd, some in remnants of airforce, navy or army uniforms, and others in old shirts and underpants; some well shaven and shorn, and some with resplendent beards. But we all gave the impression of being a jolly gang whose morale had not suffered by capture.

Judging by the crowds we attracted it was obvious that curious spectators were coming in from far afield to enjoy the spectacle, since the district was sparsely populated as, indeed, was the village itself. The whole area was given over to vineyards nestling at the foot of a high mountain range, which formed the backdrop to the camp in the distance.

The officers and guards were always eager to keep the perambulating prisoners closed up in a compact group to ensure that everyone was under close surveillance and there were constant cries from the soldiers in front to go slow - *'Piano! Piano!'* which vied with the shouts of *'Avanti! Avanti!'* from the soldiers behind as they urged on the stragglers.

In the middle of the village, the road was crossed by a cart track on the right which skirted a few houses to plunge into a large expanse of vines spreading up towards the foothills. At this point, the walk always took a left turn away from the houses and the village and then took a circuitous route to return to the camp across fairly open country.

Our escape plan was for the four of us to break ranks at the crossroads by taking the right hand turn past the houses and then to disappear at full speed through the serried ranks of villagers into the vineyards and up to the foothills. We calculated that the vines would give us cover within seconds of the breakaway, allowing the guards little time to fire effectively without risking the lives of innocent bystanders.

For our scheme to succeed it was essential to spread out the perambulating party, so that the soldiers were spaced out widely on either side and then to cause a diversion at the end of the line to distract attention just when half of the prisoners had already turned left.

The escapees in the middle of the line would then be precisely in position at the crossroads to make their break to the right.

With all this in mind it was possible to practice spreading the walkers over a number of outings before our escape attempt without attracting very much concern. The guards became less and less anxious on each occasion and were prepared to share jokes with bystanders in the village, no doubt at our expense. We estimated and fervently hoped that, when the break did occur, only one rear guard on the right-hand side would be in a position to observe it as the soldiers in front would already have turned left. It was this guard, on the right hand-side and to the rear of the breakaway, who had to be distracted at precisely the right moment.

It was planned to distract him by having two prisoners indulge in a little rough horseplay, in the course of which they would bump into him accidentally. If he was not completely distracted it was calculated he would be at least momentarily off-balance and reluctant to fire at us and possibly endanger the safety of the villagers whom we hoped would help to screen us from view. We would need only a few seconds to gain the cover afforded by the tall vines.

We calculated that once the officers in charge realised that there had been a break, they would use their soldiers to guard the rest of the prisoners, rather than disperse them to chase after us, since any weakening of security at that juncture might allow other prisoners to escape, resulting in a mass break for freedom. The Italians would obviously have made contingency plans to cover any escape attempts outside the bounds of the camp but we could only hope that we could outwit them.

At last the long awaited day arrived. We had exercised constantly, sprinted regularly, and everybody who was going on the walk had been briefed on the various vital parts they were to play. We four escapees took up our positions halfway down what we intended to be extended, straggling ranks. We wore heavy boots, quite common for our walks, and had secreted in our clothing as much food as possible without looking suspiciously bulky. Everybody was in the usual jolly mood which these walks engendered as the order to start was given.

I kept my eyes firmly on the vineyards and the inviting sparsely vegetated foothills, all the while rehearsing in my mind the direction to take when once up in the mountains which would lead to the Adriatic Coast and, hopefully, an opportunity to appropriate a fisherman's boat and cast off to a

THE AUTHOR IN PoW CAMP IN ITALY

IN STALAG-LUFT III
Standing (left to right) Garrad Cole, Goldie, Payne,
Dickie Bird (with pipe)
Gregory, Marsh, 'Ollie' Oliver, Collins and (leaning over) Brown
Sitting: Sammy Hook and Ted Lockwood

THE MEMORIAL TO COMRADES
MURDERED AFTER 'THE GREAT ESCAPE'

Above, a contemporary drawing by PoW Flt/Lt B.L. Kenyon
Below, the memorial today

Above:
ON THE WAY BACK AT LAST
Repatriated PoWs
on the Swedish ferry from
Stettin to Trelleborg
(The Author is on the far left)
September 1944

Left:
Flt/Lt A.E.V. 'Ollie' OLIVER
in 1946

landfall on the coast of Greece or Yugoslavia. I noted with pleasure that the walk was spreading out well and, although I was keyed up, the guards and everyone else seemed totally relaxed. At the crossroads we could see the usual crowd of sightseers ready with cheers and jeers. It was almost as if a holiday mood prevailed. The column of walkers was turning left. It was time to go!

I was the second of the four as we broke ranks. The people on the corner, a fairly old peasant women with children, just stood blank and uncomprehending, motionless, shielding themselves as we pushed them roughly aside. They offered no resistance as they were totally taken by surprise. They formed exactly the screen we had hoped for, behind which we had thirty seconds to disappear into the vineyards.

I took a flying leap into the vines, following my friend Pilot Officer Wilson who landed flat on his face with my heavy boots in the middle of his back. He told me afterwards that he thought one of the guards had jumped on him. Then, in an instant, we were up and away. I was only conscious of the man in front. What was happening to the other two men behind me was not for me to worry about.

I couldn't believe my luck. Not a shot was fired and our plan had succeeded. We were away! But I had not reckoned with the hazard which now presented itself. The vines were in rows supported by wires attached to stakes running the length of the vineyard and, once in a row, the sides were like walls and it was difficult to get out to right or to left.

It was only a few seconds later that I realised the danger, when I heard rifle shots behind me as bullets whizzed past my ears. I threw a glance back over my shoulder, fearing the worst, and saw a soldier kneeling about two hundred yards away, taking pot shots at me.

Thank God he was not an expert shot. In a split second I had flung myself down and, with some difficulty, crawled through the wires into another row of vines before he could target me again.

As I fell forward, the firing temporarily ceased only to be renewed almost immediately away to my left and, as I lay there in a ditch on the edge of the vineyard, I heard a series of blood-curdling screams interspersed with another volley of shots. My mind ran riot as I tried to decide what to do next to escape the fate which, from the screams, I imagined must have met one or more of my companions.

Not far from where I lay was a dry river bed leading up to the high mountain ridge which dominated the area. I decided this ridge must be my refuge. I wriggled on my stomach into the river bed only to find, to my consternation, that it was full of fine gravel which came over the top of my boots as I struggled uncomfortably and, as fast as I could, upwards and away from the vineyard.

My relief at reaching the seclusion of this deep ravine very quickly evaporated as bullets again began to streak past my head. In a matter of seconds I staggered through the quagmire of gravel, which made every movement a superhuman effort, towards the side of the ravine and pulled myself up its steep slopes and out of its confining contours into scrub which provided some welcome temporary cover from my pursuers. Moving now posed no problems and with the speed of desperation I made my way blindly forward towards the mountains. But I was quickly faced with another hazard.

The protective scrub suddenly ceased and further progress northward towards the mountains would mean coming out into the open and again exposing myself as a target. With the cunning of a hunted fox I decided not to leave the protective screen of scrub but to lie up until, as I hoped, darkness would allow me to cross the open land which now confronted me. I searched around for a particularly dense part of the scrub and burrowed rabbit-like into its ground-hugging protective mass, where I lay like a hunted animal, relaxed bodily but with my ears and eyes very much alive and attuned to the danger which threatened me on every side.

As I lay there I vividly remembered the many times that my gamekeeper father and I, armed with our shotguns, had searched similar surroundings for hapless rabbits. Now the tables were turned with a vengeance and I tasted the fear of the hunted animal.

But it was not fear as imagined by the uninitiated. It was not sickening and helpless dread. Instead, every sense was sharpened. The adrenaline was flowing. It was the hunted pitting his wits against the hunter, employing all his innate knowledge and cunning in order to survive.

I was suddenly assailed by an almost forgotten sound: the wailing of a siren, very similar to our own air raid sirens at home. The news had got back to the camp of the escape attempt, and obviously the entire neighbourhood was now being put on the alert. It was even more essential for me to be on guard as the search would quickly be intensified.

My super-sensitive hearing alerted me in the next hour or so to the proximity of several near misses as searchers came dangerously close to my hideout, but I remained rooted to the ground, immobile and unseen, not daring to look up or move a limb.

Once an armed soldier passed so close that I thought he would fall over me and I had difficulty in constraining myself from leaping up with my arms above my head in surrender. There was always the fear that a soldier, stumbling across me, might in the heat of the moment, simply shoot me out of hand rather than risk a confrontation with someone who might just be armed.

What would he have to lose?

Hour by hour dragged by with my prayers becoming more and more desperate for the cloak of darkness that night would bring, to allow me to slip away into the hills. But it was not to be. It was becoming apparent by the frenzied shouting all over the area that the hillside was being systematically combed with military precision. And then the inevitable happened. An armed soldier discovered my hideout.

I leapt up like lightning with my hands up, surrendering. He was so nonplussed and surprised that he took two swift steps back to avoid colliding with me and, whether by bad marksmanship or humanitarian instinct, fired between my extended arms, took two further paces back to ensure his own safety, pulled back the bolt on his rifle and fired again above my head.

All of this was accompanied by frenzied shouting on his part, which drowned more feeble but possibly just as frenzied protestations on mine.

All his latent Latin instincts were now truly aroused. He turned up the volume and put his rifle into the small of my back, pointing downhill towards the village yelling *'Avanti!*

Avanti!' and all the while slamming the rifle into my spine.

With every bruising jolt I was terrified that he would pull the trigger, until it became apparent that, after firing his first two warning shots, he had thumbed his safety-catch on and, in all his fury, forgotten to once more thumb it off. He was a safety-first soldier. His rifle was now only being used, with bayonet like ferocity, to impel me at the double towards his own safety zone. Nevertheless, it was enough.

It doesn't take a professional athlete to know that with your arms above your head you are not in the best position for running. In fact it is very tiring indeed. Several times on that uneven downward dash I had to stop and plead to be allowed to lower my hands but although I had reached the point of utter exhaustion any attempt to drop my hands led to a frenzied reaction.

I feared my captor would lose complete control of himself and finally pull the trigger to end what was also for him a wearying experience so I decided discretion was the better part of valour. But exhaustion knows no bounds in such circumstances and it seemed an interminable time before we reached the village where troops and civilians were massed to witness my ignominy and the end of my dash for freedom from the very point where it had started that self-same morning.

From the village to the camp was but a few minutes drive in a car, sandwiched between two triumphant looking guards who proudly delivered me to the Camp Commandant's office. Here my reception was anything but polite and I was bundled into a cell, my plea for a drink of water being waved aside. It was only when I relaxed in the cell that I realised that I had received a slight bullet wound in my left leg a little above the ankle. I had at the time felt a burning, stinging sensation for a fleeting moment, but in the confusion of effort to get out of the gully, with bullets whistling past my head, had only been conscious of the fact that my brains had not been blown out!

Two of my fellow escapees, Pilot Officer Grey and Sub-Lieutenant Neal, had fared much worse. One had received a bullet through his side which had emerged just above his hip, and he had spent several hours in his cell before being taken to the civilian hospital in Sulmona. He was discharged the next day, although it was weeks before everything had healed. It appeared that the bullet had gone through part of his intestines without piercing anything serious.

The other was the one whose piercing screams in the vineyard, had led me to believe he had suffered a fate worse than the facts later proved. He had not been able to get beyond the perimeter of the vineyard and took refuge in a small hut which was used to store stakes and canes under which he hastily burrowed. A guard quickly located him and fired a couple of shots at the ground near his head which caused gravel and stone splinters to pepper his face and neck. He was disfigured for weeks with what looked like severe acne.

The third member of our quartet, Pilot Officer Ken Wilson, had survived unscathed, the first to be rounded up.

The result of our expedition had not been successful and after fourteen days' solitary confinement we were all returned to the camp. The authorities were concerned that two escape attempts had been engineered by prisoners so soon in the history of *Fonte de Latte* and it was thought that prevention was the best kind of cure and that the ringleaders should be forthwith removed to a more secure place.

Consequently, I was confronted early one morning by police and guards and told I was leaving Sulmona within the hour together with some twenty others. The first point of call was Padua where we were deposited in a monastery where we lived in cells just as spartan as those occupied by the monks, but unlike them we were always under heavy guard and day and night surveillance.

After that, within two weeks, we were off north en route to Rezzanello in the Po valley.

Rezzanello was in marked contrast, a Nunnery, part of which had been made secure for housing a contingent of South African army officers taken in Libya by the Germans. This like the monastery was only a staging post for the 'Sulmona Brigade' we were told, but my stay there was to be anything but peaceful.

As new arrivals, we were set apart from the rest to sleep in one large dormitory and through the night we were subjected to hourly visits from an orderly officer. Bedecked in the multicoloured Fascist ribbons and sashes of his office he stomped in his shining jackboots between the beds. He was closely followed by an armed guard who ensured that his own hobnailed boots woke up anybody the officer had not aroused.

For some reason I seemed to be singled out for special treatment. It was probably only the onset of paranoia, but it seemed to me that a strong torch was deliberately being shone straight into my eyes, almost scorching my eyelids with its intensity.

A few consecutive nights of this recurrent hourly torture

was as much as I was willing to take and when the torch was once more shone into my eyes I promptly leapt out of bed and confronted the officer with a torrent of Anglo-Saxon abuse.

The ever vigilant guard sprang to the aid of his officer and I was bundled outside into a courtyard where I was quickly joined by a friend who had also objected to the harassment. We were kept out there in our scanty underclothes and bare feet in the snow which had fallen that night, while the officer reported his side of the story to the guardroom. After which he came looking for me.

He found me crouched in a corner, picking up a cigarette thrown me by a friend, and proceeded to kick me violently in the stomach. This vicious and entirely unprovoked onslaught took me completely by surprise. It winded me. I had to gasp to get back my breath. I had been treated like a dog by a scented pansy of an Italian officer and I was not going to forget the insult nor injury in a hurry.

Being sentenced to thirty days solitary confinement did nothing at all to heal the rift between myself and the Italian apology for an army, but it is amusing to look back on my soap opera of a trial before the Camp Commandant.

He was a Colonel and, of course, he was both judge and jury.

He was a tall, portly man of aristocratic mien, liberally decked out in medals and ribbons on an immaculate grey uniform. He sat rigidly at his desk stacked neatly with papers and books and with a revolver lying ominously on his blotting pad. I realised that to impress this theatrical 'Colonello' I must be as militarily correct in my bearing as he was, so I came to a very proper and exaggerated salute as I pulled up in front of his desk, and stood rigidly to attention.

This appeared to surprise him somewhat, as it was usual for captured officers to adopt a more casual attitude to show the British aplomb in adversity.

Regarding me angrily, he opened up a blue covered book on his desk, showing me its title *'Code Penale'* which he then proceeded to shout at me *'Coday Penarlay! - Coday Penarlay!'*

That's how I heard it.

Three or four times *'Coday penarlay! Coday penarlay!'* was hurled at me, as his face grew ever more puce and he slammed the book ever more violently upon his desk.

I was accused of physically attacking an Italian officer while he was on duty. The Colonello, waving his revolver, furiously shouted that the officer would have been within his rights to have drawn his own revolver in self defence.

My explanation that my actions were the result of repeated harassment by this officer did nothing to mollify him. I was informed that such action as I had taken could result in a death sentence as outlined in the Penal Code and from the way he waved his revolver menacingly in front of me, I could have been forgiven for thinking that he was himself about to carry out the execution there and then.

I stood there in front of him rigidly to attention not batting an eyelid, quite enjoying the situation. This seemed to calm him down a little. In a much more conciliatory tone, he then proceeded to relate how the Italians were a compassionate people and that my case did not warrant such a dire penalty. The sentence was thirty days solitary confinement.

Solitary confinement was something I had already tasted in Sulmona and found not too terrible. But this time it proved to be more severe, as I was incarcerated in the camp's detention cells adapted from the oldest part of the Nunnery.

My cell had an earth floor, the walls were stone blocks, and the door solid - except for a small window barred on the outside, which admitted a minimum of light into the dark interior. The furnishings were a low camp bed, two grey blankets and a bucket in the corner to serve as a lavatory. There were no washing facilities. It would not have qualified for even the most modest of ratings in a Michelin Guide.

Ablutions were timed for nine o'clock in the morning when the cell door was unlocked for an hour's exercise in a small yard, at the end of which was a washroom with long stone troughs and cold water taps. On completion of the exercise period it was back inside to partake of a breakfast of bread, margarine and sour-tasting coffee brought in by guards.

There was no more food until the evening when after the second hour's exercise prescribed by the Geneva Convention, a bowl of pasta and a bread roll with the nauseating coffee completed the diet.

The two breaks during the day were eagerly anticipated - the sun was warm and the fresh air was champagne after the damp smells of the dungeon.

Although the courtyard was surrounded by high walls there was always something to hold one's attention. Cheeky sparrows would hop over the rooftops while, of particular interest, were the spiders, guarding their strategically placed webs in the corners of the brickwork. These spiders nested in small holes and cracks on the sunny side of the courtyard wall, spinning webs of no more than a centimetre across the apertures. Each spider remained in its hole motionless and patient until an unsuspecting fly tempted by the warmth radiating from the wall settled, to its peril, on the predator's web. A lightning strike from the spider and the fly was in the larder. . .

These simple interests helped relieve the tedium of solitary confinement.

In my cell, I was constrained either to lie down on the bed or pace the few steps up and down across the earth floor.

Time was something one had to forget. It passed so slowly that after a few days one was confused as to how many days had gone by. It was necessary to scratch a mark on the wall to signify the passing of each day and that was when you noticed all the other scratch marks.

The first few days seemed never ending and the empty days ahead stretched out into an eternity. In the solitary confinement cell one certainly had the privacy denied in the camp, when one's fellow prisoners could quite easily get on one's nerves.

But solitary confinement was a very heavy price to pay for it.

6

Gavi

THE NUNNERY, we knew, was only a staging post for the 'bad boys' and soon after completing my sentence we were on our way to a veritable fortress at Gavi. This was a small village high in the pre-Alps north of Genoa and, incidentally, not far from where I was shot down. I had travelled the whole length of Italy to Rome and Sulmona and now I was back in the north.

The fortress had the air of a medieval castle, perched high on a rocky crag which rose perpendicularly eight hundred feet or more above the village. It had been used in the first World War to house Austrian prisoners, since when it appeared to have been left uncared for and uninhabited. The approach to the fortress was conventional, across a dry moat spanned by a drawbridge, beyond which the entrance was guarded by a portcullis of medieval proportions.

When approaching and entering any new camp, it had become second nature to us to make an instant assessment of its possibilities for escape. We quickly glanced this way and that, taking everything in, doing our best to memorize all that we saw. For once we were truly and completely inside the opportunity to have a second look would be gone.

On this occasion, as we passed through the massive portals

of our new home, the portcullis dropped with a loud clang of finality behind us, a sound which echoed hollowly along the dark cobbled tunnel which lay ahead. Beyond, we emerged in a courtyard almost as dark as the tunnel itself, around whose perimeter was a series of drab stable doors with small heavily barred windows between them. These derelict stables were to be home for the 'bad boys'.

Now we knew the worst.

Each stable was furnished with four camp beds and the dark grey coarse blankets did nothing to improve the decor. There was one large cupboard; no stove for heating; while the rough stone walls had been recently whitewashed. Washing and toilet facilities were located in a distant block primitive in the extreme. No conventional water closets with seats, there were simply holes in the floor over which one had to crouch uncomfortably.

At the other end of the courtyard was our dining room, a rather grand appellation for a place with bare stone walls, a flagged floor and rough pine tables and benches. Here the camp meals were served up twice a day. This dining room could have been described in the words of Estate Agents worldwide as having 'a breathtaking view'. Two windows, heavily barred, looked down on to the village eight hundred feet below the sheer cliff of granite. Had it been possible to remove the iron bars which had been sunk deep in the stone to resist even the impact of a battering ram, one would have needed a parachute to effect an escape.

About thirty officers were the very first guests of the management, all of whom had been branded by the Italians as *'pericolosos'* - dangerous people. Discipline was strict; roll calls took place day and night; the usual privileges, such as the facility to send a monthly letter home were withdrawn. Records at the Imperial War Museum show that the Italians had allocated fourteen of their officers and two hundred and forty other ranks, including special police, to guard the one hundred and eighty prisoners-of-war who were eventually incarcerated here but the Swiss Red Cross were never notified that this special camp ever existed, so they never visited it, nor did we ever receive Red Cross parcels.

After two weeks in Gavi I was summoned to the office of the Camp Commandant. Completely mystified as to why I had been sent for, I was abruptly informed that the thirty days solitary confinement I had just completed at Rezzanello had not only been confirmed by authorities in Rome, but that such a serious view had been taken of my crime that a second sentence of thirty days solitary confinement had been added to the first.

The Senior British Officer promptly lodged a complaint and insisted that thirty days was the maximum sentence that could be imposed under the terms of the Geneva Convention. We were quickly disabused and advised that Italian regulations required only a week's respite after a period of thirty days solitary incarceration, after which time any remaining sentence had to be served.

As there were no Red Cross visits to Gavi, our captors knew no complaints could reach Switzerland and they had complete freedom to do what they liked to us.

At Gavi there were only two prison cells in the solitary confinement yard, both of which were then occupied. I was suffering from a severe attack of diarrhoea at that time, the dreaded prisoners' scourge, but in spite of my protestations and appeals to let me wait until I had a cell to myself, it was all to no avail. The chance of having to share a cell for a few days with another prisoner might appear attractive, but the thought of having to hog the bucket almost exclusively day and night was an acute embarrassment.

I willed my brain to ignore signals from my bowels. It took a great effort but such is the power of the mind over the body that it worked, and the diarrhoea magically subsided. After three days with my companion I was left alone with twenty-seven days really solitary confinement ahead and, curiously, I said goodbye to my cell mate with no regrets. At least I would now have the bucket to myself!

I knew the ritual of solitary confinement by now, how to keep track of the days and how best to pass endless hours in the half light of the cell. Sleep was a great blessing and the nights were as peaceful and as quiet as the grave. Except for a daily energetic two hours of exercise, I could put myself into a sort of trance for hours at a time, and the days like the nights passed by without incident. But it was nonetheless a mind-numbing experience, coming so soon after the previous thirty days incarceration.

Back in the camp, my sentence now behind me, we were visited regularly by an aged Italian Roman Catholic Priest in his round black felt hat and long black cassock, belted tightly around the waist. He spoke very good English, had a lively wit, and gave the impression that his sympathies lay with the Allied prisoners rather than with the aspirations of our Fascist captors and their German comrades in arms.

Many Italian Catholics did not support the Mussolini gang

and the way he had tied their country to the coat-tail of the Nazis, but they had to be discreet. From the priest, we gleaned the whole history of the fortress which, according to him, was a labyrinth of tunnels, sealed up caves and secret passages. At one time it had been a monastery, and legend told of a secret tunnel, dug out by the monks, winding its way down to the village below to permit the more licentious brethren access to warm female comforts during the long cold winter nights.

This tale of secret tunnels fell on very receptive ears and produced much serious thought as to how we could confirm their existence and use them in our future escape plans. We would gaze for hours from the dining room on to the village below, a sight which always beckoned to us tantalisingly, starved as we had been of our liberty for so long.

I mused how lucky the animals were which grazed peacefully and freely on the banks of the little stream which trickled through the village, and the dogs which playfully chased each other in the narrow street. While gazing on this scene I made a vow that should I ever be free again I would never worry whatever befell me. I realised that personal freedom is every human being's greatest possession. To come and go at will, to walk in the city, to climb a mountain, to follow a river, or to simply stand and stare and drink in the glory of the world all around is everyone's birthright.

So escape to freedom was an obsession and in the camp everyone was a fitness fanatic. We were all acutely aware of the fact that strength and stamina were essential to a successful escape, particularly in the mountainous country around Gavi. But first one had to get out of the fortress. . .

Every inch of the walls, floors and ceilings of our prison

was examined minutely in the hope of discovering something which might help us escape.

Then something struck me. On closely examining the walls of the cell where I slept with my three other Sulmona friends it became obvious that the top two feet of one of the walls had been plastered separately from the rest. It topped the rear wall of the cell, furthest from the door and, when I tapped it, it sounded hollow. And so, to a lesser extent, did the wall beneath it. Neither, by any manner of means, gave out the solid sound of a wall hewn out of the living rock as most of the rear walls in the cells appeared to be.

Was it possible that behind this wall was a space, which at one time had been divided from the rest of the cell by a partition finishing some two feet from the ceiling? This would account for the disparity we could observe in the plastering. We decided to probe this possibility closely.

The first step was to make a small hole in the wall about eighteen inches above floor level, but before undertaking this we spent a week with our ears glued to the wall, day and night on a rota system, to make sure that if there was a space behind it that space was not occupied at any time.

When we had satisfied ourselves on this point it was easy to gouge out a small exploratory hole and keep it hidden from view behind the cupboard. Through the hole it was possible to make out a series of cubicles, shadowy in the darkness, but there appeared to be no exit. The vacant space appeared to be an old disused lavatory previously entered from the cell in which we were living.

The space had probably been sealed up by the Italians when they provided a central toilet block and it was hard to hide our excitement at the possibilities that this discovery created.

It took only a few hours to enlarge the hole sufficiently to allow one of us to wriggle through to investigate further. I was designated the operations boss, and discovered that the area had been completely sealed off with a heavy iron grille in the ceiling which was about eight feet above the floor.

Only a glimmer of light fell down into the area from the grating but within minutes of entering my blood ran cold and I was rooted to the spot as I heard the unmistakable sound of heavy footsteps approaching. I began to wonder whether I was hearing the footsteps of the ghost of a prisoner who had been sealed up behind the walls centuries ago!

As I stood transfixed, I glanced up at the grille and could dimly make out the legs of an Italian sentry as he passed over the grating. His boots were so large they almost covered it as he slowly and heavily passed by, only to return a few minutes later on his patrol.

I instinctively pressed myself up against the wall. I didn't need to consciously stop breathing. The sudden fright had left me breathless and my knees a little weak. The echoing steps receded some twenty paces, when the guard turned about and passed over the grille once again.

It was apparent that above the grille there was an external rampart, patrolled constantly. But the guards who, so far, were quite unaware of our activities, could be quickly alerted if we put a foot wrong. It was imperative to maintain strict silence and to be extremely vigilant.

We had the advantage that we knew of the presence of the guards overhead, whilst they had no reason to suspect our activities below. As soon as my composure returned I gently eased my way quietly back through the hole to tell my excited comrades what had transpired and we all agreed to proceed cautiously.

During the following week we maintained a continual surveillance of the comings and goings of the guard overhead. Whenever the sentry passed over the grating the precise time was meticulously recorded to see whether the guards followed an exact routine. The patrols were continuous but none of the sentries ever made any attempt to examine the grating or to try to peer through it. To them it was obviously the cover of just another drain, and they had no reason to anticipate any trouble from it.

It was doubtful if any of the Italian security officers would have a comprehensive plan of all the structural alterations which clearly had been made within the fortress over the years. Nobody would know precisely what lay behind those rocky walls which appeared so solid and impregnable. The Italians would be reasonably confident that the place was secure. Although they were aware that their British prisoners were very ingenious, they also knew that pneumatic drills and thermal lances were not in a kriegie's armoury.

Our main concern was to keep our activities secret; we had heard on the grapevine that in one of the lower levels in the fortress some prisoners had broken through into a sewer and had been forced to swim through raw sewage as a result. We hoped our project would be more sanitary!

After a week we were ready to push on.

By that time a careful examination of the space to which we had gained access confirmed that it had indeed been a lavatory and that it had once possessed an external door, which had been bricked up. We decided to investigate. The only tool at our disposal was a small rusty piece of iron which had been prised out of the wall in the courtyard, so progress was bound to be slow. But there was no immediate hurry. Winter had set in and heavy falls of snow in the north and in the mountainous surroundings to our prison discouraged any attempted breakout before the arrival of spring.

We set to work. Two of us took it in turns to attack the wall with our makeshift tool while number three kept his eyes and ears wide open to warn of the arrival of the sentry on the grating above, when work had to cease momentarily. At the slightest sign of any alarm or disturbance above, or within the rest of the fortress, we would scuttle back to our cell and quickly move the cupboard into position to conceal the hole in the wall.

On some days security made it impossible to make much progress, however the winter months were never dull as we dreamed of the possibilities that lay ahead.

Eventually the bricked-up door space in the lavatory wall was breached. It had been like chipping one's way out of the Cheddar caves with a penknife, but we finally gouged out a hole wide enough to wriggle through. Beyond was a much smaller cavern hewn out of solid rock, at the far end of which a rusty old pipe of considerable dimensions disappeared into earth at a steep angle.

It was possible to squeeze down alongside the iron pipe without disturbing too much soil for a distance of about fifty feet when the pipe disappeared into a solid mass of concrete. A major problem was to get a little light into the working area, but we hadn't forgotten how to fashion a rudimentary lamp using olive oil from the cookhouse and passing a string wick through the cork of a bottle into the oil.

The concrete encasing the pipe was a setback but it proved to be merely a temporary one, giving us time to size up the situation.

We calculated that the pipe must at that point either discharge itself into a large chamber or perhaps this might be where it broke surface on the slopes of the hillside on which the fortress was built. For the catholic priest's stories of the monks and of their secret passages lent credibility to a burgeoning belief that we had, in fact, discovered one such passage which, at a later date, had provided a ready made conduit in which to lay this large pipe when the sewerage system was improved and modernised. Wasn't it possible that where the pipe now disappeared marked the end of the monks' tunnel, where they had made their exit on to the rocky hillside above the village?

Spring had almost arrived. The snows of winter no longer provided an obstacle to hold us up. It was decided to tunnel as close to the concrete as possible in the hope that we might break through to the outside world, even if we did find ourselves high on the hillside. If the monks could make their way down the slope from that point it should not present us with any insuperable problems.

At this time we were scraping away round the concrete into some fairly soft gravel so progress was speeded up considerably. Very soon in the gravel there appeared evidence of fibrous growth which encouraged us to believe that not so very far above us there were trees or vegetation of some sort.

In previous tunnels the soil at depths of over eight feet was always damp and completely sterile, so we had high hopes that our months of effort were about to reach a dramatic conclusion.

Just how dramatic that conclusion was to be, and exactly how imminent we could not foresee!

Early one morning when we'd had a particularly promising dig the day before, with roots becoming more and more abundant, hordes of Germans, heavily armed, suddenly swarmed into the camp without warning. We were told that the camp was to be evacuated next day. It was unbelievable!

Previously we had seen a few German officers in the camp, but they had aroused no suspicions. The visitors were usually officers of the elite German Panzer divisions from North Africa, satisfying their curiosity with a sight of English officer prisoners of war at close quarters. They were educated and polite and behaved impeccably. Now we were confronted by a rabble of German troops highly excited and in a very aggressive mood.

We feared that their sudden arrival meant that our next prison camp was going to be inside Germany itself. The Italian priest was to be seen running around and he told us that the Germans had moved heavy transport into the village during the night and that their troops surrounded the camp so that escape was impossible. All the Italian administration staff and guards had been removed and the Germans were in complete control.

With our escape plans advancing to fruition this was a shattering blow. Twenty-four hours before I'd had high hopes and now every one of them had been dramatically dashed. It would be impossible now to complete the tunnel so we had to think of something else quickly.

We thought it was possible that the Germans would not have totally accurate details of the number of prisoners held here. Or, at least, that was what we hoped. For the only plan we could come up with was to hide ourselves away to escape evacuation into Germany, and it seemed to us that our tunnel was the best place. So we made up our minds that as soon as orders to evacuate were given the four of us would disappear into the tunnel after persuading our mates next door to push the cupboard against the hole in the wall and then to jam one of the beds tight against the cupboard to reinforce its position.

We had high hopes of success and decided at this late stage to let the Senior British Officer, an Australian Army Brigadier, know that we would not be turning up for the evacuation next morning. The Brigadier, however, demanded that we show him our proposed hideout and then promptly told us that he would be joining us there next morning.

We were dumbfounded. We explained to him that the Germans might possibly be prepared to pull out with four junior officers unaccounted for, but in no circumstances would they leave without the Brigadier, the Senior British Officer. If he insisted he would spoil our own chances of escape and our remonstrations became heated as we told him precisely what we thought of him with no respect for his rank.

Early next morning there was pandemonium everywhere as prisoners were hounded out of their cells with shouts of *'Aus! Aus!'* and herded into the lower courtyard by German troops with bayonets who looked eager to use them. We made one last desperate plea to the Brigadier who was now in our room, having by this time removed all his insignia of rank from his uniform. We told him it was more than the lives of the German officers were worth to leave without him, the prize prisoner. But the more we beseeched him to join the rest of the prisoners who depended upon him for a semblance of legal protection the more adamant he became.

In this sudden crisis he suddenly looked fearful and small and, stripped of his insignia he was no longer our Senior British Officer but a figure of contempt.

In desperation I played my last card and told him that if he insisted, then he could hide up there by himself without any assistance from us.

That was the final word. The Germans were approaching our cell quite prepared to winkle out the reluctant prisoners with their bayonets. The Brigadier bolted through the hole, we slammed the cupboard up against the wall and left him there to his own devices, our immediate concern being to duck the rifle butts and bayonets and to join our comrades assembled in the courtyard.

Frantic attempts were being made to count the prisoners and, it was now obvious that with Germanic attention to detail, they had in fact secured the camp records before dismissing the Italian administration.

The German officers made no effort to halt the aggressive behaviour of their troops which got more and more menacing as the prisoners tried to stall their efforts to account for everybody in the camp. Soldiers were dispatched back to various compounds to forcibly eject any recalcitrant stragglers and sporadic gunfire began to echo around the courtyards.

They were making it quite clear that they were prepared to

tolerate no nonsense and expected prisoners to obey orders or face the consequences.

It appeared that they had a time schedule for evacuating the camp, and were as nervous as if they expected a British landing in the vicinity to come to our aid. The prisoners already assembled were being marched outside after being meticulously checked off by rank and number against the camp register, and German agitation could be seen to increase as it became evident that the Australian Brigadier had so far eluded them.

Outside the camp a large convoy of heavily camouflaged lorries was assembled and, one by one, under the guns of the guards, the trucks were quickly filled up with prisoners. The vehicles had heavy canopies as roofs, while canvas flaps at the rear and sides helped enclose the prisoners safely. Most of the troops were trigger-happy young Nazis, well disciplined and drilled products of the Hitler Youth, revelling in this opportunity to demonstrate their fanaticism. At that juncture it would have been suicide for anyone to attempt to escape.

As the lorries filled up, four armed guards took their positions at the back of each one, and they slowly moved off in convoy, to the accompaniment of rifle fire within the fortress. The Germans had seemingly accounted for most of the prisoners, but had sent in more troops to prise out the few who obviously were holed up there, and loud explosions testified to the ferocity of the operation.

As the last remaining remnants were winkled out to join us, bedraggled and stunned we were given graphic reports of German troops lobbing grenades into drains and other likely spots to flush out those prisoners who were reluctant to leave.

The Brigadier would have been very exposed to this drastic action, with the grille on the ramparts just over his hide-out.

Despite everything we could not wish him a violent end. Perhaps he had unwittingly saved us from some disaster we had not been able to foresee.

7

Into the Reich

THE GERMANS WERE DETERMINED to get the convoy moving and the lorries were soon on their precipitous descent to the village and thence northward into the mountains.

The villagers, startled by the aggressive appearance of the German troops and the sound of explosions and small arms fire emanating from the fortress, waved us cautiously on our way. But whether they were waving out of sympathy for our plight or relief that normality could now return to their village was a question we couldn't answer, even if we'd had the time. We all had something else to think about.

For everybody realised that there was still a chance to engineer an escape as we drove nearer to the Swiss border and that as soon as we reached Germany opportunities would be few and far between.

As our lorry slowed down to negotiate a sharp bend two prisoners abruptly rolled backwards under the canvas side-flap, disappeared over the edge of a steep mountainside and were swallowed up in the thick scrub. It had all happened in the twinkling of an eye, as if they had been catapulted out of their seats at the moment when the lorry lurched violently, momentarily leaving the guards unsighted as they clutched their Schmeisser sub-machine guns and held on to their precarious positions at the back of the lorry.

The convoy rolled on relentlessly and finally arrived at a small railway station hidden in a valley some twenty miles north of Gavi, where we were ordered down.

There the Germans made it plain that they were in no mood to treat the prisoners as 'officers and gentlemen' for as the train drew up into the station we realised that we were to be transported in cattle trucks similar to those used in France in the first World War where *'Hommes et Cheveaux'* were boxed in together. There were no seats, no toilets, simply straw scattered on the dirty floors and very little of that!

As the train came to a halt there was one last desperate effort to escape which could only be described as suicidal. A prisoner slid down on to the track between the platform and the trucks, scrambled up the other side and plunged across the neighbouring field. We could see him running in full view as we stood there helplessly, only to see him cut down by a hail of bullets. He was punched forward and upward by the impact to sprawl in a motionless heap.

We were all stunned and sickened by the slaughter and left the German officer in charge in no doubt that we would have liked to have lynched the killers who, quite unmoved, now began using the butts of their rifles on us to get us into the trucks as quickly as possible.

It was an extremely warm day, so I quickly seized the opportunity to scramble up to the far end of the truck and ensconce myself directly under a small iron grille in the wall, a position which I calculated would be more light and airy when the doors were closed. We were packed into the truck like sardines. There was just sufficient room for all to sit on the floor but it was absolutely impossible for everyone to lie down at the same time. When the train finally chugged slowly out of the station, we hoped that the total absence of water and food and even basic toilet facilities was an indication that the journey was to be a short one.

Hours later the train came to a halt, and in the darkness the doors were slid open to admit two German officers who climbed into the truck, kicking prisoners out of their way while they unceremoniously tossed around tins of sardines and loaves of black bread. I immediately thought of Christ's feeding of the five thousand with loaves and fishes as they sat at his feet, but there was no Christian compassion for us as the Germans contemptuously kicked their way quickly out of the truck again. It was clear that their objective was to bully and demoralise us into submission.

These particular German officers were members of the *Feld Gendarmerie*, the German Military Police, whose job it was to ensure that nobody flinched from his wartime duties, however unpleasant or inhuman the task might be. They had authority to instantly execute, by shooting or hanging, anyone even suspected of desertion, or refusal to obey a command. They were thugs hated by their own people. But they were there to see that Nazi ideology reigned supreme within the German army.

The doors were slammed shut as they paid no heed to requests for an opportunity to leave the truck briefly to relieve ourselves. We were expected to behave like the animals for whom the trucks were intended, and to answer the calls of nature accordingly. The tins of sardines and the bread were our first and last meal of the day.

The truck became intolerably stuffy and as we all could not stretch out together, it was agreed that we should take it in turns to lie down, first one half of us for an hour or so and then the other. As the night stretched on it became impossible to ignore the demands of nature and the empty sardine tins were requisitioned to hold the urine. When bowels had to be evacuated, it became a matter of a tin at both ends, and spillage was widespread as the train rocked and rolled along.

I very quickly realised that the advantages of being directly beneath the grille were outweighed by the serious disadvantages. The contents of the two tins had to be got rid of outside, and there was only one way. After skilful swirling between the tins the resultant semi liquid mess had to be dextrously tossed through the grating immediately over my head.

No matter how loudly I protested the grille was used continually throughout the night and try as I might it was not possible to twist myself sufficiently far away from it to escape the consequences. By morning I had begun to resemble a milk chocolate soldier but I smelt like a skunk!

I was covered from head to foot in urine and excrement. It was in my hair, in my beard, it was everywhere.

Some of my fellow travellers tried to make light of my predicament by giving voice to what in our Mess days was considered an amusing ballad *'Sweet Vio-lets - sweeter by far than roses, covered all over from head to foot, covered all over with. . . Sweet Vio-lets'.*

This verse was repeated *ad infinitum* until at a signal from the conductor the last two words, *'Sweet Vio-lets'*, became *'Shit!'*.

On Mess nights this last word was bellowed out with great gusto by the more inebriate members. It was only in drunken revelries that such a ditty was tolerated, but whenever I have heard it in the years which have followed my wartime experiences it has always instantly brought back the most unsavoury memories for me.

Soon after daybreak the train halted and everybody was bundled out and marched to a tented compound at the back of a small railway station. We discovered that we were in Graz just over the Italian border in Austria. In peacetime, Graz was a ski resort and now, in the morning sunshine, it was especially beautiful as the snow-covered peaks glistened in the distance. It looked like the outskirts of Paradise after that hellish journey and the air was like champagne. . . except anywhere near me!

My discomfort switched my thoughts from champagne to water. Thank heavens there was plenty of that and, at the standpipes I was able to wash from head to foot. But it was not possible to do more than rub at my clothes to get rid of the smell as there were no facilities for drying them and we only had what we stood up in.

The foul stench could not be completely eradicated, but a prisoner who had no change of clothing for years never smelt like someone promoting aftershave, so I was no longer treated as a leper. By kriegie standards, I was no longer unclean. But in the afternoon when the journey was recommenced, I understandably gave the area close to the grille a very wide berth.

The Germans must have been a little taken aback at the insanitary state of the trucks that morning, for when we boarded them again we found that they had been hosed out. Fresh straw lined the floors and everywhere was pervaded by a strong smell of disinfectant reminiscent of freshly cleaned stables. After a few hours the train was halted again to allow prisoners who wished to relieve themselves to do so by the side of the track, under the watchful eyes of armed guards who covered the whole length of the train.

It was a fairly peaceful scene with prisoners' trousers dropped down over their ankles until a young Yugoslav RAF officer, perhaps sensing that he was near his birthplace, decided to make a break for it. Choosing his spot and his moment and - he thought- out of sight of the guards, he rolled down the bank to be instantly cut down by a burst of machine gun fire. He sprawled there spread-eagled over the bushes and immediately a siren on top of the train howled its warning that trouble was afoot, not that the kriegies, taken by surprise and hobbled by their trousers around their ankles, were in any position to attempt a mass breakout. But the guards stirred into action by the earsplitting siren began firing their sub-machineguns into the air and urging the prisoners to get back quickly into the trucks, while the train started to move slowly forward, adding to the pandemonium.

With my trousers still down I struggled to keep up alongside the open doors of the moving truck, while those still inside tried frantically to pull comrades up to safety. The guards running alongside the trucks attempted to close the doors while the prisoners outside were still fighting to get on board. I was pulled up in the nick of time by strong, willing hands as the train began to move faster.

Several prisoners unable to reach their allotted trucks were mown down by the guards and left lying there, half naked by the side of the track as the train gathered speed. Momentarily I lay on the floor of the truck realising how near I had come to death and I felt a sickening revulsion as I visualised friends of mine writhing in their last agony mercilessly murdered by the trigger-happy guards. We loathed everything German.

To add to our plight we realised that the further we were transported into the Fatherland, the further we were being removed from any hope of escaping what lay ahead, which was beginning to look like an eternity of this same inhuman treatment. It didn't bear thinking about.

In the evening we were subjected to a repetition of the feeding arrangements of the previous day. It was all so sordid and escape had now become an obsession. If only it was possible to prise open the doors a mass escape could be attempted when the train was forced to slow down, as it did frequently during the night, but the doors were heavily barred and bolted from the outside.

A rugged New Zealander named Bishop had succeeded in wrenching off a piece of the metal strips which reinforced the floors to prevent cattle stamping their way through them. We now had a primitive tool and hurried discussions took place as to the relative virtues of trying to escape through the floor or the roof of the truck. As the floor was heavily reinforced it was decided that the roof offered the better chance, since the metal strip could be forced between the tongued and grooved roof timbers more easily.

In no time a hole had been gouged in the roof just above the iron grille, sufficiently wide to allow a man to pass through. The excitement that generated was electric, as the real possibility of escape had suddenly been presented to us. Quickly decisions were made as to the order in which individual prisoners would take their chance as soon as the train slowed down enough to allow somebody on the roof of the truck to slither down on to the track.

When the train had stopped for us to attend nature's call we had come to the conclusion that the guards accompanying the train were in a separate compartment at the rear. There was a possibility that troops were also stationed up front but we hadn't been able to check. The fresh air now rushing in through the hole in the roof intoxicated us and made us oblivious to the danger of what we were contemplating.

We calculated that some would be bound to succeed; if death came to others, we trusted it would be a quick and a happy release from a very uninviting future. It was decided that Bishop, who had provided the tool and done most of the work making the hole in the roof had earned the number one place. I was lucky to be number five in the pecking order. What food there was left in the truck was divided amongst those prepared to take their chance, as there were some who, for reasons best known to themselves, could not, or would not, brace themselves up for the venture.

The plan was to pop out through the roof, quickly slip down on to the track and, aided by the darkness, melt into the mountainous countryside. It all seemed inviting and so easy that our excitement reached fever pitch as we waited for the train to show signs of slowing. Then all of a sudden it was all go.

Bishop could contain himself no longer. He slipped up through the hole and disappeared swiftly from view, as number two quickly followed him. In seconds number three was being hoisted up by eager hands when a hail of machine-gun bullets blasted the roof of the truck and the scream of a siren filled the air.

What had gone wrong? Nobody knew! Had Bishop and his number two got away, or had they all been gunned down as they clung to the roof awaiting an opportunity to drop down on the side of the track?

We realised as we lay there on the floor quite stunned by events, that the guards must have had a vantage point at either end of the train to enable them to see over the roofs of the trucks. We should have known that they would be bound to remain vigilant throughout all of the night.

The train was quickly halted and the doors to our truck were wrenched open as a dozen guards, highly agitated and voluble, took up predetermined positions. Several German officers jumped in, their pistols at the ready, while *Feld Gendarmerie* with sub-machineguns peered inquisitively into the interior to assure themselves that most of the prisoners were still there.

The German officers went berserk kicking their way amongst the prisoners sitting on the floor and screaming abuse and obscenities as they fixed their gaze on the gaping hole in the roof. In a matter of minutes the guards produced hammers and nails as though they had been expecting all along to have to carry out such repairs and made good the damage as best they could. We were warned in no uncertain manner that if the roof was tampered with again in any way the whole truck load of prisoners would be shot. There would be no survivors!

Frequently during the journey the train was halted so that

the roof could be inspected and we didn't dare test the sincerity of their threat. It was clearly not beyond the bounds of their villainy to claim we had all been shot resisting their efforts to prevent a mass escape.

Early next morning we arrived in Munich. We saw the name of the station as we spewed out of the trucks on to a temporary platform prepared to receive us. Here we were, ironically, in the very city where in September 1938 Neville Chamberlain had been mesmerised by Adolph Hitler into thinking he was carrying back to England a piece of paper guaranteeing 'peace in our time': a pact to avoid the very war we were now fighting.

Trains were running into Munich at what we imagined must be the peak morning rush hour and passengers were crowding to get a glimpse of the prisoners on parade. From the windows of the high-rise buildings overlooking the station, people were focusing binoculars on the unkempt British officers surrounded by a tight cordon of troops. The scene had quite obviously been staged for the benefit of the German civilians and the intended humiliation of the British prisoners. And Munich had been especially chosen as the prime spot for us to attend a call of nature in the full glare of publicity. There had been no efforts to screen off the area.

Over open trenches, our lavatory 'seats' were long poles suspended horizontally on which we were expected to perch. We balanced precariously with trousers dropped down round our ankles, much to the amusement of the German public.

As I sat there, I recalled a leaflet I had seen which had been handed out by the German Propaganda Ministry to all civilians in targeted German cities in an effort to pour scorn on the British leaflet raids. These, which had opened the air war when bombs would have had more effect, had urged the Germans to surrender to avoid real air-raids in the future. The German leaflet portrayed RAF aircrew with their pink bottoms protruding over the sides of the planes, which they were wiping with the leaflets advising the Germans to surrender. Such was German humour! It was now calculated that the German people would be amused to see at first hand those pink bottoms depicted on their leaflet, while at the same time inflicting further indignities on their prisoners. For our part, we sat there quite serenely on our perches waving genially to the inquisitive onlookers to show them that it would take more than an attempted humiliation like this to shake our morale.

As we left Munich we reluctantly said goodbye to a city bathed in sunshine and bustling with activity, a sight which we had almost forgotten during our incarceration.

We thought the next stop on our train journey would never come. All we could do was doze uneasily as we rattled on endlessly into uncharted territory and we wondered what was going to happen next in this increasingly disagreeable saga. Such speculation ended as the train abruptly came to a halt in the middle of nowhere: no station, no building in sight. We were in the middle of a large fertile plain, well cultivated but with not a single tree to break a landscape which stretched away into the hazy distance.

Raucous shouts of "*Aus! Aus!*" and rifle butts beating the sides of the trucks indicated that our captors would be grateful if we left the train. Other trains of wagons were stationary further up the track spilling out their human cargos of prisoners whom now we were to join.

We were lined up, a seemingly unending, stinking straggle of unkempt humanity, but we kept up a steady stream of banter to lift our spirits and to show the Germans we were not daunted by our predicament. There must have been about fifteen hundred of us as we were given marching orders and the crocodile began to wend its way slowly away from the trains across along a well worn track across the plain.

Our guards were ever trying to speed up our progress but we were in no hurry to be confined again, either within a truck or a PoW compound and we did our best to delay things. We were enjoying this walk in the clean fresh air as much as if it were a Sunday school outing.

Sauntering across the plain we finally began to see a cluster of huts in the distance, still some way off so well camouflaged that they merged into the drab landscape as if planted there by nature's hand. The cluster of huts soon took on the familiar aspect of a large bleak complex surrounded by barbed wire, with watchtowers and perimeter floodlights. Despite this, as we approached, it was a welcome sight after being confined for so long in those insanitary cattle trucks. The promise of a bed to sleep in, running water and lavatories, however primitive, with the prospect of being able to stretch our legs, even if it was behind barbed wire, was a blissful thought. The camp could not now be reached quickly enough. It was like a beckoning oasis. Soon we were halted in front of the administration building.

The first ordeal was to strip down to our trousers and pass in single file before a squad of formidable looking doctors to receive an anti-typhus injection. The doctors in their long white coats turned out to be captured Russians and they punched their hypodermics into our chests with the force of boxers attempting a knockout. The needles looked as thick as knitting pins and were just as blunt. They were never replaced and more and more force had to be applied in order to puncture the skin.

Immediately in front of me in the queue was the tough Canadian paratrooper who, in Sulmona, had made our blood run cold as he told how he had slit the throats of some Italians guarding a bridge before he was captured. As soon as his turn came for inoculation, and even before the needle had actually made contact with him, he keeled over in a faint and had to be carted off.

Elsewhere in the long queue, other 'strong men' were also dropping like flies. My turn next. I steeled myself against the body blow and, hopefully, was rendered typhus free.

Next we entered a large high-roofed shed built like a hangar. And here we had to strip off completely and put all of our clothes and our few small personal belongings on to a conveyer belt. As we stood there naked, another squad of white coated Russians armed with heavy-duty electric hair clippers descended upon us and in seconds denuded our scalps of every last vestige of hair with the dexterity of expert shearers. Beards were similarly erased. We stood there like a flock of newly shorn sheep. Divested of hair and clothes everyone looked alike. It was even difficult to pick out one's friends.

But our ordeal had only just begun. Instructions were broadcast that our clothes had gone on to be fumigated to rid them of all fleas and lice and that we would now personally undergo the very same cleansing process in the fumigation chamber which opened before us. It was tiled from top to bottom, with row upon row of pipes, like sprinklers, criss-crossing the ceiling.

We were packed inside like sardines and no sooner were the steel doors closed, than we were enveloped, spluttering and choking, in an eye-stinging vapour which made breathing difficult and blinded us temporarily.

It was fortunate that, at that time, none of us had heard of the mass extermination of Jews in German gas chambers. Had we done so, our captors would surely have had a riot on their hands. We were inside the chamber for only a few minutes, but they seemed like hours. And then the doors opened and, coughing and spluttering, we struggled out to collect our fumigated clothes and belongings.

As we pulled on our clothes we felt very unsteady. The gas had been very strong and undoubtedly lethal to any lice or bugs with which it came in contact. Or so we thought. But on opening my bag of small belongings to check nothing had been pilfered, I saw, sitting on top of them, quite the largest cockroach I had ever encountered, very much alive and well.

Like the rest of us it was understandably a little unsteady on its pins, but it was moving its wings with obvious delight at having survived an experience which, as far as it was concerned, was supposed to mean certain death.

I did not have the heart to crush it. I simply brushed it aside and by doing so I hope I helped perpetuate a breed of cockroaches which would be immune to extermination by gassing and live to infest every home throughout Germany.

Soon after our fumigation we were split up between the

various compounds. It was apparent that the huts had only recently been vacated and that little effort had been made to clean them out and make them ready for our arrival. Which was how I came to discover a small canvas haversack under a corner camp bed which I had selected close to those of my ever faithful friends. No doubt it had been accidentally left by a former inmate in a hurried evacuation.

I examined its contents excitedly. A dirty old razor was discarded, but other small items were kept. Particularly, most valuable of all, a small quantity of dried peas, sufficient to fill a teacup. We had never had peas before in our prison diet, and next day they were soaked and mashed in with the daily ration of potatoes and shared with my two closest friends. We all agreed it was the tastiest meal we could remember and the haversack remained with me till the end of my incarceration.

As soon as we had laid claim to our spaces in the hut it was time for bed. We were exhausted by travelling and our experiences after arriving in the camp. Soon the whole building was reverberating to the snores of massed prisoners, thankful for the luxury of wooden beds and of somewhere to stretch out full length and sleep. That sleep was deep at first, but towards morning, as our initial fatigue began to wear off, we were rudely awakened by the activities of hordes of bed bugs.

Most English people have never experienced bed bugs as bed fellows. Now we had that experience. The whole hut was really alive with them, and they had uninterruptedly gorged themselves on the kriegies sleeping the sleep of exhaustion. My body was covered with bites which had swollen into small blisters, and it was literally impossible to place a match head on any unaffected part of my face and neck both of which had become swollen beyond belief. The irritation was intense.

By daylight the whole hut was in an uproar. The beds were being violently upended as the mattresses which were large rustic sacks filled with paper were flung on to the floor before being jumped on by the crazed prisoners in their efforts to rid themselves of the bugs. Pandemonium reigned by the time the Germans opened the huts and the whole day was spent in debugging. The sacks were torn apart and the seams turned inside out, for it was here that the bugs slept off their night-time feast.

It was incredible. Every inch of the seams, when explored, was lined with the reddish brown insects, from which our blood spurted out everywhere as they were crushed. It was a filthy, revolting and nauseating business.

As soon as the mattresses had been cleaned, attention was focused on the wooden bed frames. Wherever there was a joint in the woodwork, or even so much as a hairline crack, there were the bed bugs seeking refuge. It was difficult to dislodge them from such inaccessible hiding places until we finally discovered the ultimate weapon. We burned them out. We passed lighted paper spills across every crack and crevice in the woodwork and thank God it worked.

After such a busy day's activity we might have expected a good nights sleep but it was not to be. Within a few hours of lights out the bugs struck again. We may have incinerated hundreds, but thousands were left, and they were hungry. The whole wooden building was heavily infested with them and they were on the march. They came up from between the floor boards and out of the joints in the wooden walls of the huts. They could be seen swarming across the ceiling before dropping down, airborne, to attack the occupants of the beds below.

It was like a horror film. Their assault was relentless. We killed one and two more took its place. There was no stopping them. Next morning after vehement protests to the Germans we were turned out wholesale into the compound while the sanitation gangs moved in to fumigate the buildings. But those bugs had acquired a built-in resistance to chemical killers and we were never entirely free of them.

Many of us put the legs of our beds into empty food cans filled with water as a basic protective device, for the bugs still hadn't learned how to swim. But we remained at the mercy of the airborne division that crept along the ceiling and dropped adroitly on to their victims. Against these we had no defence.

For our first few days in the camp, our preoccupation with bed bugs occupied our minds to the exclusion of everything else and we hadn't taken in what was happening around us in some of the other compounds separate from our own.

At the end of those first few days many of our bites had turned septic and had caused such serious inflammation of our arms, legs and face that some rudimentary medical treatment was necessary and I was included in a batch of about twenty-five prisoners marched out of the compound under guard to the medical block some distance away but still inside the confines of the camp.

What we were then to witness was totally unbelievable and is hard to describe. It ranked with the atrocities of Belsen and the other mass death camps which most people outside Germany only knew existed at the end of the war. It was only then that the horrific deeds of the Germans were exposed in all their barbarity to the outside world as these terrible places were overrun by the Allied forces.

This prisoner-of-war camp in which we unaccountably now found ourselves was, we learned later, the infamous Muhleburg into which the Germans had herded many thousands of Russian prisoners-of-war. Unlike all the other combatant nations, the Russians had never signed the Geneva Convention. This, administered under the auspices of the International Red Cross, required signatories to observe minimum standards of humanity in dealing with prisoners of war.

The Japanese could, and did, sign the Convention and then went on to dishonour that pledge and the entire Japanese nation by their savage and uncivilised treatment of captives later. Russia had indulged in no such hypocrisy.

The Russians guaranteed no basic rights to their prisoners and the Germans, when dealing with the Russians, whom the Nazis categorised as sub-human, were only too glad to follow the same policy.

The compound in which the Russian prisoners were confined lay between the one which held the recently arrived British prisoners and the medical block, so it was impossible to screen it from those of us being marched past for treatment. It was the stuff of nightmares. The compound seethed with masses of hooded skeletal figures, padded out with any rags of clothing available to keep themselves warm, so that their silhouettes assumed grotesquely weird shapes. Hardly any of them appeared to be wearing boots. Their feet were encased in filthy rags upon which they shuffled slowly around like animals inside their cage.

As we approached they scuffled in waves up to the wire of their enclosure, their eyes sunken and expressionless deep in their skulls. They were like a crowd of corpses as they slowly and deliberately jostled with each other for room to poke their emaciated claw-like hands through the wire. Their palms were outstretched in silent supplication.

We were marched past at a quickened pace, the German guards keeping their stony gaze firmly fixed upon us to avoid the terrible scene.

The Russian prisoners uttered no sound. Possibly they recognised us as British officers and, however insanely, hoped that we could bring them deliverance from their unbelievable plight. But we could do nothing. We had come upon this scene so suddenly that we simply could not believe it. It was mind boggling and as horrific as if we had been marched into a cemetery where suddenly the corpses had risen, mummified, from the graves.

How the Germans could inflict such inhuman treatment on one group of prisoners while showing concern for a few Britons suffering nothing more than mild blood poisoning it is difficult to comprehend. Unless we accept that the entire nation, with very few exceptions, had swallowed the Nazi creed in its entirety and thought the Russians truly sub-human and completely expendable.

Some Dutch prisoners who we encountered working as conscripted medical orderlies in the camp had even more gruesome stories to tell. The Germans were systematically starving Russian prisoners to death and some two thousand had perished of hunger the previous winter. Their only food to be shared out between them was a daily load of swedes, which they had to eat raw as they had no cooking facilities. The swedes were dumped just inside their compound and the cart disappeared as quickly as it had arrived to limit contact with the prisoners to the minimum.

Close by, the Russians had been ordered to pile up the bodies of those who had died during the night. The corpses were loaded by their compatriots on to a low cart like a haywain, which was then dragged, under guard, by some twenty or so living corpses to a spot about two miles from the camp. There the dead bodies were thrown into a large lime pit with no ceremony. The quicklime burned up the bodies rapidly with little smell and prevented the outbreak of plague.

Whether the Germans deliberately denied the Russians mechanical transport to pull the wagon as a final act of barbarity or whether they thought that in allowing the 'living' corpses to bury their comrades was a compassionate act, one will never know.

As we were returning from the medical block after hearing these horror stories we were just in time to witness one of the funeral processions disappearing across the fields. The sight of animated corpses shuffling at a snail's pace alongside the death wagon was as macabre as any horror film sequence I have ever witnessed and one which even time will never erase from my mind.

After this it was clear why the Germans had shaved and fumigated us with such thoroughness on our arrival at the camp. With the hundreds of dead and dying and with hordes of bed bugs capable of spreading disease, they knew they were sitting on a time bomb which could explode at any time.

In retrospect, why British prisoners had been brought into this particular camp and allowed to witness what was going on there is difficult to understand. At the time this display of man's inhumanity to man cast a deep depression over all of us. For we didn't know then that, as far as we were concerned, Muhleburg was only a temporary staging post.

Soon we were to be leaving this camp of horrors, and when that time came we certainly didn't enjoy the thought of being cooped up in cattle trucks once again.

However, we were consoled by the knowledge that, thanks to the Geneva Convention, whatever our fate, it could never, ever begin to compare with that of our Russian allies in Muhleburg.

8

Stalag-Luft III

AFTER TWO DAYS AND NIGHTS once more living like animals in the cattle trucks our journey ended. We had arrived in Poland at a small town named Sagan, home of the now well known Stalag-Luft III immortalised by the screen epics *The Wooden Horse* and *The Great Escape.*

Stalag-Luft III had been constructed specifically to house RAF officer aircrew. It was a German priority to securely hold RAF personnel whom they intended to use as a strong bargaining point in negotiations when the war ended to secure the release of their own personnel in Allied hands.

This was not what we were told by the Germans at the time. Indeed we were threatened with a sinister "You will never return home. When the war is over you will be put to work in the salt mines in Silesia and you'll stay there until you die!" Which wasn't a very happy prospect as workers in the salt mines over a prolonged period developed incurable ulcers as the slave labourers in the Third Reich knew to their cost.

To keep up our spirits we would laugh at these threats and indicate to the guards who made them what their fate would be immediately the war ended by passing an extended finger across our throats and then getting quickly out of their way. They didn't seem to like the idea of having their throats cut and tended to react very violently.

From the railway station it was a march of about a mile to the camp, constructed deep inside a forest of pine trees, where eight large low huts made up one of the four compounds, North, East, South and West, plus administration block. All the buildings were of wooden construction and the four compounds were about a quarter of a mile apart, each surrounded by high barbed wire fences and overlooked by tall observation towers manned day and night by armed guards. Searchlight beams swept the compounds continuously after dark.

Whilst the layout of a prisoner-of-war camp is now as well known as that of a Butlins, having been depicted on television and on film so many times over the years, few people will ever have experienced in the whole of their lives the chill feeling of despair and the sense of utter abandonment felt by prisoners as they entered such a drab, hostile and inhospitable environment. My own arrival in Sagan had, however, more than an element of surprise. For there, standing inside the gate amongst the inmates already installed, was the Senior British Officer, Group Captain Massey, who had been the commanding officer at Abingdon during part of my training.

Group Captain Massey, who had been a First World War pilot, must have been the most senior officer ever to have been shot down on a raid. Such senior officers had long since been forbidden flying on operations and corralled into 'more important' administrative duties. Perhaps he had been on a very special assignment but more likely an uncontrollable urge to once more take part in active combat had been his ticket to Stalag-Luft III.

The sight of him standing there immediately brought to mind his last words spoken to me at Abingdon. They were "Oliver! Is it *worth* it?" These words which were certainly appropriate to my present situation had originally been uttered in very different circumstances.

It was early in 1940 and I was sitting in the Officers' Mess at Abingdon as I had been given twenty-four hours off duty after a series of injections. From my seat in the bay window where I was writing a letter home, I would glance up from time to time to take in the aerial activity around the station. Suddenly, I was frozen to my chair in horror, simply transfixed.

A Whitley bomber was heading straight for the Mess, only a few feet up, with one wing trailing and showering sparks off the driveway. A second later and it had smashed into the building, demolishing part of the roof and narrowly missing the window where I was sitting. The whole building shook under the impact.

In seconds everyone in the Mess was out there. The plane was engulfed in flames and the grass in front of the building was well alight. I scrambled across it to get close to the plane hoping that I might be able to assist the crew to escape, if any of them were still alive. At that moment there was a huge explosion. The petrol tanks in the wings had gone up and the effect of the blast was like a violent kick in the stomach. To add to all the noise and confusion the ammunition in the plane began to explode like infernal fire-crackers.

Fire engines and ambulances were soon on the scene and in no time at all the plane was covered in a mountain of foam. But there were no survivors. All five members of the crew had been cremated in the blaze.

As the flames were being brought under control our attention switched back to the Mess whose roof was burning furiously. A wing had cut through it spraying it with petrol which had instantly ignited. There was a concerted rush back into the building and, as other fire tenders poured water on to the blaze everybody worked frantically to save as much as could be salvaged. Furniture, pictures, carpets and curtains, plus the contents of the bar, soon littered the front lawn.

Group Captain Massy was there supervising the operations as young officers fell over themselves to earn his approval. As the roof began to collapse it was necessary to fall back into the large entrance hall. It had already been stripped of most of its contents when, in the last frenzied moments, my eyes alighted on the head and antlers of a massive stag which adorned the wall, over the stone fireplace. Its glass eyes were already reflecting the glare of the flames which were about to singe its very hair.

It had such an appealing look, abandoned there when virtually everything else had been removed that I had to save it. In my enthusiasm I grabbed the nearest chair and grappled with the heavy weight; which came away from the wall suddenly, sending me and the chair flying.

The ceiling in the hall was already collapsing as I started to pick myself up, still grasping my trophy. There was the Group Captain issuing his last orders to everybody to leave the building. He stood above me as I heaved myself on to my feet and it was then he yelled "Oliver! Is it worth it? Get Out!"

Of course, I realise now that it was not worth risking my

neck for that of a stuffed stag, but I simply could not resist that mute look of appeal. I couldn't leave the old boy to burn, and I hope that he still graces the wall over the fireplace in the hall of the rebuilt Officers' Mess at Abingdon.

Seeing the Group Captain so unexpectedly inside the gates of the camp had sparked off those memories of the hazards of life even in the comfort of an Officers' Mess at home. Now, once again, the grim realities of my present predicament took over. Luckily my two close friends from Sulmona, 'Greg' Gregory and 'Tiny' Grey, were still with me and we quickly got ourselves established in neighbouring bunks in the same hut.

Both of my friends were married men, while I fortunately had nobody to worry about except myself, and I began to notice that, as time passed, both were getting progressively more morose and withdrawn as they speculated on when, if ever, they would be home again. The future appeared to be bleak but one had to concentrate on living each day as it came and ignore any thoughts of the future. There was no place for hopes or for dreams. Live day by day, that was the only way to survive.

We had no sooner settled in the camp than we noticed one of our room mates had become deeply depressed. He dreamt day and night that his wife had fallen for a German Officer PoW in England and that they were having a torrid affair. It was impossible to convince him that such a liaison was sheer fantasy. He couldn't get the thought out of his mind.

One day when the huts had been secured by the guards for the night he tried to force his way out towards the wire perimeter and was only restrained with difficulty from what would have been a certain death. A few days later when everybody in the hut was asleep he disappeared and we were only alerted to his absence when all hell was let loose in the compound. Searchlights were blazing, guards screaming at each other from all quarters and guard dogs were on the rampage as a fusillade of shots rang out.

We peered through closed shutters and saw our comrade coned by the searchlights, hopelessly entangled in the barbed wire, his arms and legs spread-eagled as if nailed there on a cross. His death would have been instantaneous but it spread even more gloom and despondency through the hut amongst those of us who had shared close contact with him.

As the days dragged on, the Senior British Officer had an unenviable job in keeping up the morale of his men, and we were constantly reminded that although we were prisoners of war, we were still on active service and subject to his military discipline. Those of us who still had uniforms to wear were expected to keep our buttons shining and to present ourselves as officers whatever the circumstances, to show our captors that we could never be demoralised or defeated.

As Stalag-Luft III has already been featured in many books, films and television programmes I'll do my best to avoid 'overexposure' by recalling here only those incidents and episodes with which I was closely associated.

Inside the camp, the vista was stark and dreary, but winter brought very heavy snows which instantly transformed the scene particularly once the sun had broken through. Then everywhere sparkled like a white wonderland. But beneath the surface, the camp showed every sign of having been thrown up in a hurry.

For example, between all the huts there still remained the stumps of huge fir trees which had been felled and used in construction. The stumps poking up out of the hard frozen ground were our only fuel supply, but first they had to be dug out by our own effort with the picks and axes which the Germans supplied by day and with great efficiency took back again in the evening.

Whether we froze to death in our sleep or survived the intense night-time cold depended solely on the joint efforts of the inmates of each hut. It was extremely exhausting work only undertaken under pressure for our survival.

We were short of food. The effort expended in wrenching the stumps up and out of the iron-hard frozen ground took so much out of each of us that, at the end of each day we were exhausted. Every night the temperature dropped alarmingly and we were hard pressed to keep the voracious iron stoves heated for just a few hours.

When the day's ration of wood was burned out it was necessary to take refuge in our wooden bunks and cover up with the lone light blanket provided. There was no ritual of undressing for bed. Every bit of available clothing was donned and sleep was possible only thanks to the balaclavas and greatcoats provided by the benevolent Red Cross. Luckily I had been able to hang on to my fur-lined flying boots which, as far as my feet and legs were concerned, were better than hot water bottles. The temperature in the huts dropped so low that, by morning, the water in the large pitcher we used to leave continually on top of the stove was frozen solid. We were frequently told that the previous night's base temperature had been forty degrees below zero!

In the winter mornings we were loath to turn out of our huts for roll call and stepped out into the deep snow wrapped up like mummies. We were however able to strip off some outer layers of clothing as the day progressed and the sun came out fitfully. It was necessary to stimulate the circulation by walking briskly around the compound just inside the tripwire in twos or threes, which became known in camp jargon as 'being on the circuit'. Consequently by midday it was possible to take off sufficient clothing to keep arms free for the more vigorous exercise of digging out our daily fuel supply.

The stumps were there in profusion but nobody had the energy to dig out anything like the quantity of wood to keep the huts really warm throughout the long winter nights.

As the war progressed, and the German lines of communication were flattened by Allied bombing, it became difficult to move food around the country, and understandably the prisoners of war were the first to feel the pinch. In an emergency they were expendable. Not so the German troops and factory workers. In Stalag-Luft III rations were one loaf of bread per week per man, plus a few ounces of margarine and a hard slab of jam which resembled a jelly pack.

Breakfast was supplemented by German 'coffee': a large pitcher of an ersatz brew made from roasted acorns. Alternatively, we might be offered 'tea' made from pine needles. Both were equally obnoxious without milk or sugar - but they were hot and never refused. At midday each hut received a pitcher of soup made from barley in which sometimes, a few pieces of meat the size of a dice would be floating around; but never enough of them for everybody to have a piece. Food rapidly became such an obsession with us that a roster had to be kept to ensure that everybody was equally treated throughout each week.

The bread we received was black rye, allegedly bulked out with sawdust. It tasted sour and stomachs and palates did not take kindly to it. The routine was to slice the weekly loaf as soon as received into twenty-one pieces to provide three per day: one slice with jam for breakfast, one slice for lunch with the soup and the last slice of the day with margarine and jam in the evening. Though we were anything but enamoured with the bread, to try to supplement our food we always stationed one of our hut mates near the bread slicer when it was issued with instructions to sweep up all the crumbs as everybody cut up their ration. Several handfuls could be gleaned in this way and made a useful addition to our soup ration.

A British doctor in the camp calculated that our average food intake was less than one thousand calories per day even when supplemented by the occasional Red Cross parcel. He warned that energy should be strictly conserved, yet we had to expend loads of it digging out wood simply to keep warm. It seemed a harsh choice - hypothermia or starvation!

There was one unexpected bonus to stump digging. The rotting roots and the surrounding soil were often infested with large white grubs, waxen, each about the size of a man's little finger. These we found were delicious when cooked in an empty tin over the stove and provided the less fastidious with tasty and much needed protein.

Years later I have come across similar grubs when digging my garden in Surrey near to the conifers. I have often been tempted to sample the taste of this English variety of our Stalag delicacy, but have left them on the bird table where the robins and blackbirds gobble them up with the same glee we long ago used to exhibit.

As food got more scarce and rations were reduced yet again, the Senior British officer lodged strongly-worded complaints with the result that we were suddenly treated to a large load of potatoes dumped just inside the main gate as a one-off gesture. The potatoes were in such an advanced state of decomposition that they were almost reduced to a stinking jelly. They were obviously the remains of a Polish farmer's crop which had suffered the full rigours of the severe winter frosts.

Despite the wretched stench emanating from the heap it was eagerly surrounded by the kriegies pushing and shoving, each keen to salvage something edible, while at the same time trying to avoid falling into the filthy mess.

Our particular foraging party succeeded in collecting about twenty small potatoes before the heap was picked clean like a carcass by a horde of filthy vultures.

Even after being washed frequently the potatoes continued to smell. So much so that during daylight they were kept outside the hut - albeit under a very close watch. It was only at night that they were suffered inside the hut to prevent their disappearance. Over the next few days, these potatoes helped to augment our meagre fare and reduce our pangs of hunger, but they did little for our health.

Then the camp suffered from an epidemic of dysentery, and the *Aborts* (row after row of thunder boxes contained within a large, stinking fly-ridden wooden hut) were besieged continuously by suffering kriegies. Queuing for the *Aborts* was a daily ritual. At all hours prisoners could be seen shuffling forward silently in ordered rows until their time came to occupy a vacant thunder box. As could be expected one's time on the box was taken up with much badinage and cries of "Come on for God's sake! You've been there for ages!" and sometimes one would obligingly hop off the seat temporarily to allow a friend to take over when his dysentery could no longer be controlled.

The *Abort* block served some eight hundred people and consequently the pits beneath it had to be emptied frequently. The unfortunate Russian prisoners were allotted this task, aided by the 'Honeywaggons', horse drawn tanks into which the effluent was manually pumped. The stench during such an operation was indescribable. There were no bees around that brand of honey. Only hordes of disgusting flies!

The waggons were each the size of a normal petrol tanker, and two prisoners conceived the idea of using one as a means of escape. The Russians on a waggon were persuaded to take only half a load of effluent, to allow the two men to clamber inside when the attention of the German guards was distracted and stand in the contents up to their knees. Crude gas masks were constructed as the fumes inside the tanker could prove to be lethal.

The two men planned to remain in the tank after it had been pumped dry outside the confines of the camp and arrangements had been made for Russian soldiers employed in the hospital to secrete some clean clothes near the parked vehicle under cover of darkness. At nightfall the escapees were to grab the clothing, wash themselves in a stream and make good their escape.

Precisely what happened to these two men we never discovered. Rumours circulating via the hospital were that they'd had to bale out of the tanker early as the gas masks had proved ineffective and they had also been in danger of drowning in the effluent as it slurped around inside the tank on the very uneven ground outside the camp. It was an ingenious idea but one never likely to be repeated, although escape plans were forever being discussed during the long hours we spent locked up in the huts.

It was a primary requirement that before putting any escape plan into action it should have the approval of the Senior British officer whose job it was to ensure that any new plan would not jeopardise the success of any scheme already in progress.

From time to time the Germans would react to their ever-present suspicion that escape plans were afoot and hordes of armed troops would suddenly be rushed into the camp in armoured troop carriers. The soldiers would charge into the huts like maniacs yelling *"Aus! Aus!"* and woe betide anyone who didn't heed the warning and make a speedy exit to avoid their bayonets and brutal rifle butts.

The soldiers having emptied the hut would then proceed to systematically tear everything apart. Floorboards would be prised up, clothing and bedding would come flying out of the windows and doors. Every action was calculated to convince us kriegies that any confrontation with the authorities was something which did not pay and that we were far better off opting for the quiet and submissive life.

If the raids took place in the winter it meant spending

many hours out in the open, often not properly clad as no warning of the onslaught was ever given. The Senior British Officer would lodge his protest after each assault on the huts, but this only seemed to bring further reprisals down on our heads.

Sometimes the raids were carried out by members of the Gestapo who would comb the huts with meticulous precision, looking most sinister in their long black leather coats hiding all but the ankles of their heavily studded jackboots. Any taunts or jeers from prisoners met with an instant and violent response and the result invariably meant a spell in the cooler to give the offenders time to reflect.

9

The Wooden Horse

SOON AFTER I ARRIVED IN STALAG-LUFT III a fellow prisoner approached me to ask if I'd join a new escape scheme which was being worked on inside the camp. That fellow prisoner was Flight Lieutenant Tony Barber who, some twenty-five years after the end of the war, became Chancellor of the Exchequer in Ted Heath's Conservative Government and who was later appointed Chairman of the Standard Chartered Bank in London. In Stalag-Luft III he assisted the Senior British Officer as co-ordinator of all escape activities.

He was a very live wire and must be given a lot of the credit for the success of the daring and ingenious escape described at length by Eric Williams in his best-selling book *The Wooden Horse* which later became a highly popular film. I was very flattered by his invitation and readily accepted, little knowing exactly what he had in mind - that I was to play a very minor part in the support team which assisted Eric Williams, Michael Codner and Oliver Philpot to make their clear 'home run' and become the heroes of the Wooden Horse saga.

While walking around the circuit one day, Williams and Codner had hit upon the idea of constructing a contemporary Trojan Horse, a modern version of the famed beast of Greek legend which had deceived the defenders of Troy. Theirs, they thought, might just fool their captors and they were right. The Germans duly fell for it.

They gave their consent for the prisoners to make and to use a vaulting horse within the camp, ostensibly to improve the P.T. classes. It was a box horse, made out of wood, with sloping sides, more or less the shape of a small ridge tent, with a flat, padded top for vaulting over. The sloping sides were all enclosed, but the bottom of the box horse was open and this enabled two men to secrete themselves inside it, supported by apparently innocuous strengthening struts, and to be carried unobserved and set down on a predetermined piece of ground.

The plan was to use the hollow vaulting horse to shield and to hide the covert activity of the men inside as they began to dig a tunnel beneath it.

Previously, every tunnel had to begin beneath a hut. What else could provide the necessary cover? But this had meant an inordinately long excavation before breaking surface outside the camp. The prisoners' huts and the perimeter wire were intentionally set a long way apart. Consequently, a daunting amount of time and a colossal amount of energy had to be expended in any ordinary tunnelling attempt. Many, many months could go by - a year or more, even - and all the time the dangers of tunnel collapse and the ever-present risk of discovery grew.

Small wonder that Eric Williams' and Michael Codner's idea was hailed as *'Brilliant!'*

The vaulting horse was to be carried to the same precise spot every day. It was to be set down well away from the huts and fairly near to the trip wire which marked the inner boundary of 'No Man's Land', the area which separated the prisoners from the barbed wire entanglements and observation towers guarding the camp's perimeter. No Man's Land was a prohibited area which no prisoner might enter. Anyone disregarding this rule could expect to be shot.

The surface of No Man's Land was fine soil, raked over regularly, so that anyone setting foot on it, by night or by day, left a trail which would be readily spotted by the guards patrolling the perimeter fence or on the top of the observation towers spaced around the perimeter eighty to one hundred yards apart.

Prisoners were checked off regularly, at morning and evening roll calls, and there were also surprise turnouts at irregular intervals, sprung on us without any warning and intended to catch any plotters off-balance. Line-ups for roll call were always in the same place between the huts and the wire and it was in this area that the spot for the vaulting horse was selected, at a point precisely equidistant from two of the observation towers.

It was there that, as soon as the guards on the towers had had time to accept the Wooden Horse at its face value and had got used to seeing daily P.T. classes exercising and vaulting close to the wire, tunnelling began.

It called for a meticulous attention to detail. Sand covered the surface of the ground on which, each day, the horse was set down. The first job was to remove an area of the sand in order to sink a trapdoor into the earth beneath and then, below it, start digging out a vertical shaft. All the excavated soil had to be packed into cloth bags and stored within the horse until it was carried back to the cookhouse each evening with its workers inside it. And before that could happen, the trapdoor had to be covered with sand again and the area smoothed down.

It was appreciated that it might be difficult to make the surface of the disturbed sand appear completely normal and this was duly dealt with. At various times during the day, about twenty officers joined the P.T. classes, providing the excuse for the horse to be brought out and it invariably happened that, after some hours of classes, P.T. finally degenerated into horseplay which scuffed up the sand over a wide area, even as the vaulting horse was being carried away by four stalwarts from the last group, straining at the two stout poles passed through holes in its sides.

Warning of emergencies either in tunnelling or out in the camp, could be passed by a system of prearranged signals tapped on the side of the box horse. There was always a P.T. instructor virtually glued there, helping novice vaulters to clear it and constantly listening out for any sounds from within. There were many alarms, but no real disasters.

When I accepted Tony Barber's invitation to join the scheme I did not realise that I was being recruited as a gymnast. If I had, I might well have cried off. My injured back still gave me a lot of pain from time to time and the starvation rations we had experienced at Muhleburg had left all who had endured them seriously weakened. So much so that I found long daily periods of enforced gymnastics particularly exhausting.

But we gymnasts really weren't there for the good of our health. Nor were we there only as an excuse for the horse. We each had a well defined part to play in any emergency which might ever arise and, having once been entrusted with the job, it would have been treachery to attempt to cry off. In this beehive of activity I had become trapped as a worker, nothing more, slaving away daily with no hope of sharing the spoils.

The digging continued slowly month after month. With winter approaching there was no incentive to speed up, except that when winter finally arrived the soil would become rock hard and snow would prevent the excavated soil being surreptitiously distributed around the camp by the expert 'soil dispensers'. These officers had long cloth tubes hidden inside the legs of their trousers into which the soil extracted from the tunnel was introduced. The dispensers would mingle with the other prisoners milling around and at an appropriate place with their hands in their trouser pockets, pull a piece of string to release a retaining safety pin at the base of the tube and allow the soil to slowly dribble out around their ankles, where it was scuffed about by the milling hordes and dispersed for ever.

Snap roll calls offered the greatest hazard to the success of the operation. At such times extra German troops would descend on the camp without warning, and it was not possible to get the diggers up to the surface in time, so after they had pulled down the trap door they had to be left underground, and the vaulting horse moved quickly aside.

Roll calls were never made easy for the Germans who were notoriously bad at counting heads at the best of times. Every day there were always a number of prisoners too ill to leave their bunks and all sorts of ruses were employed to make this number difficult to confirm.

The prisoners were lined up in blocks which corresponded to their respective huts, and the German NCO's seemed more preoccupied with pleasing the German officer conducting the roll call and getting it over quickly, than making absolutely sure that the numbers were correct. Prisoners would move around - slip from one rank to another and generally make a correct count impossible and the NCO would be compelled to save face and report "All present and correct" at the same time as his fellow enumerators were saluting, clicking their heels and giving the all clear.

This organised daily shambles made roll calls a hit and miss operation, so it did not present too much of a problem to disguise the fact that two people had sometimes to be left underground. In the morning and in the evenings, the two diggers would always be on parade.

Once winter really had us in its grip the tunnel had to be closed up and with no excitement to stimulate minds, life became more and more depressing. The flow of Red Cross food parcels on which, in this camp, we had come to depend, had suddenly ceased, without explanation. The Germans were rolling the Russians all the way back to Moscow and the war and our incarceration looked likely to stretch on forever. Although they continued to wreak increasing havoc on German industry from the air, the Allies were suffering defeat after defeat on the ground. There was little enough here to raise our morale.

A wireless set had been fashioned and hidden within the camp on which the many talented RAF wireless wizards could tune in to the BBC's special news broadcasts to occupied Europe. While the set was in operation it was necessary to have security scouts on alert to ensure no Germans were around. The news would be passed by the scouts from room to room and hut to hut verbally, never in writing, to ensure that no bulletins would fall into German hands and thus confirm their suspicions that a radio set was concealed somewhere within the camp.

The set was dismantled daily after the reception of the news, and the integral parts separately secreted to ensure the whole radio could never be confiscated. If any part was discovered by the Germans, there would always be a backup component immediately available or fairly quickly obtainable from external covert sources.

Contacts outside the camp were made through the camp hospital, located outside the four barbed wire compounds and which was staffed at the lower levels by Russian officer prisoners. The link was completed by the daily visits of Russian prisoners to the various compound cookhouses to bring in the rations under German guard. It was possible, using these contacts, to operate our own underground postal service between the compounds.

The German security men who forever roamed inside the compounds searching and probing everywhere, particularly under the slightly elevated huts, were known to us all as 'ferrets', and some of them had over the course of time been cleverly compromised. British prisoners were forbidden by the Senior British Officer to seek to bribe a guard without specific authority. Certain key prisoners with a command of the German language had been appointed go-betweens to tempt German guards to their rooms on perishingly cold days to partake of a cup of real coffee from a Red Cross parcel, which for the German soldier had become a long lost luxury.

Cleverly, slowly and deliberately the cup of real coffee had become a prized gift, as had a small tablet of English soap or a small bar of chocolate. Particularly soap and chocolate, which could be passed on as presents to wives or girlfriends, were worth their weight in gold to a deprived German guard.

And once a German had accepted a gift he was firmly in the hands of an elite team of British officers, a fish hooked and ready to be landed at will.

There would come a time when it was necessary to ask favours of the German guards who had so naively accepted gifts. Protestations that such favours were impossible to provide and that, if found guilty of fraternising with a prisoner, a death sentence was mandatory, only made the guard tighten the screw upon himself. The requests for the favours could not be fobbed off. Veiled threats would follow, until the hooked fish gave up the struggle and could be quietly reeled in.

Various components for radios, likewise small cameras for making false identity documents, were all smuggled into the camp by these terrified accomplices, who were given more contraband to dig them in ever deeper under the guise of rewarding them for the risks they had been forced to take.

There were times when the blackmailer and his victim became bosom friends again, and cups of coffee would be offered without any immediate demand for a *quid pro quo.* Then the German would hope and pray that he had satisfied his blackmailer once and for all, for once hooked, these collaborators must have been haunted night and day by the dreadful fear that, by accident or design, they would, sooner or later, be exposed by the blackmailer to the German authorities and find themselves in the hands of the Gestapo.

Most of the guards were C3 category men, not suitable for any kind of service more active than that of prison camp duty but, having fallen into the hands of the blackmailers, they would gladly have volunteered for service in Russia to escape the nightmare which they were involved in. Better to be killed on the Eastern Front as a hero than shot as a traitor at home!

The prisoners had their nightmares too. The news from the BBC did nothing to dispel despondency. Churchill had announced in Britain's darkest hour that, in spite of reverses, the Allies would fight on regardless, confident that victory would finally come, were it were to take two years, five years or even ten.

Whilst this was obviously calculated to demoralise the German civilian population which was suffering increasingly from the Allied bombing, the thought of another two years incarceration was unbearable and ten simply could not be contemplated. Prisoners were beginning to show signs of severe depression. Some had become suicidal and were removed from the camp, to mental institutions we could only hope!

In the severe winter most of the prisoners were huddled inside the huts trying to keep warm and passing the time playing cards or reading material supplied via the Red Cross.

Kind people at home had responded to appeals from the Red Cross for books for the PoWs, but I fear some saw the appeal as an opportunity to rid themselves of books they found dull or boring rather than selecting those which might give comfort and pleasure to prisoners of war. I managed to acquire a most unlikely contribution to the cause, a fairly hefty tome entitled *Trustee Law and Accounts* by Rankin Pegler and Spicer. I read and re-read it until I could almost quote it verbatim. To many, it might not have appeared very inspiring, but I was grateful to the kind donor for giving me something to exercise my mind, although I didn't realise at the time that it was to serve me so well. After the war I was posted back to Trinidad by Barclays Bank where, coincidence of coincidences, I was in charge of their Trustee Department in Port of Spain!

Lighter reading took me through the complete *Herries* series by Hugh Walpole, in normal circumstances something which I doubt I would ever have found the time to attempt. But the eventful life of Rogue Herries lifted me out of the cruel environment in which I found myself and transported me in spirit above and beyond the barbed wire which bodily fenced me in.

Apart from keeping mentally occupied, personal hygiene was a bit of a problem. There were few facilities to keep clean, and the lice and the bed bugs were our constant companions. In summer it was possible to improvise regular showers as jugs of water would quickly warm up in the hot Polish sunshine. In winter, at infrequent intervals, we were marched block by block outside the camp under armed guard to a large shower room, next to the Administration building, where we had to make the best of a very bad job.

The Germans supplied no soap and were almost as niggardly with hot water which was switched off almost as soon as it was turned on. In the brief moment that water was available, it was a matter of survival of the fittest to get positioned under a shower head, no holds were barred and in the mêlée one had to carefully protect one's more sensitive parts from painful aggression.

The weakest members of the party, pushed out of the way, would give up the fight physically and instead indulge in verbal abuse, aimed at embarrassing those they could not contend with by making unflattering comparisons of their private parts. I hold this truth to be self evident: all men are not created equal.

The shower block also provided an opportunity to search for and rid ourselves of parasites. Just to be physically outside the compound was a bonus. Even those unable to get a shower counted it worthwhile to be there and to join in the banter.

Many of us had been lucky enough to obtain a pair of woollen longjohns supplied by the Red Cross, but laundering them in winter was impossible. During the intense cold they made an excellent lining to trousers, but drying problems prevented either being clean and fresh. I was wearing boxer shorts when shot down and since they were more easily washed and dried I was able to wear them next to my skin all the year round.

It was a great tribute to Courtaulds, then the fabric market leader, that my boxers survived over four years of continuous washing and wear. In summer they even functioned as shorts and gave me an edge over the other stark naked sunbathers.

Health was always a concern, although generally the camp was free of flu and other epidemics associated with winter. No doubt these germs found it hard to survive or multiply in such cold conditions. My back injury was always a source of concern and digging out tree stumps for winter fuel on top of all those endless days as a 'gymnast' had done nothing to improve it. Sleeping in the ramshackle contraption my bed had become after I'd surrendered bed boards to shore up the tunnel and replaced them with string, was the last straw that broke this camel's back.

Suddenly sleep became almost impossible as the pain increased unbearably. And if being horizontal was bad, being upright was much, much worse. Sometimes I was unable to get out of bed for days at a time and had difficulty in persuading the guards to leave me alone. It was their wont to unceremoniously eject any suspected malingerers from their beds for roll-call and I had to convince them that my problem was real. To make matters worse, during my incapacity, I developed acute food poisoning. I could only lie in bed moaning, much to the embarrassment of my room mates who were helpless to assist me in any way.

After a run of sleepless nights for everyone, the Senior British Officer finally persuaded the reluctant German authorities to give me proper medical attention and I was strapped tightly to a canvas stretcher and carried through deep snow to the hospital block a quarter of a mile away.

The guards put the stretcher down from time to time to rest awhile, and the uneven ground pressed into my spine so painfully I could not suppress shrieks of agony, much to their embarrassment. They were very glad when we reached the hospital.

10

Outwitting the Germans

THE CAMP HOSPITAL was controlled by a young German physician and surgeon, who was assisted by Major Matthews, a British doctor, who had been captured by Rommel's men in North Africa. The hospital orderlies and kitchen staff were Russian officers, compelled to work as their country was not a signatory to the Geneva Convention, which expressly forbade captured officers being forced to work for their captors. There were ten patients to a ward in the timber built hospital and each enjoyed the luxury of a camp bed, while the large iron stove which radiated warmth in each ward made them appear as inviting as rooms at the Ritz.

There were no roll-calls in hospital, and the food, although very basic, was brought to the wards by Russians who, here at least, seemed to be treated humanely and were cheerful in consequence. Life began to take on a new dimension, sleep and more sleep, punctuated by visits from the German doctor with Major Matthews in his reassuring British army uniform always in attendance.

The Major was a kind affable man, and as the pain in my back gradually eased and I recuperated we would match our skills at chess as he sat by my bedside. As my health returned I was keen to assess the chances of escape, which I felt would be easier to accomplish in the relaxed hospital atmosphere, but Major Matthews advised me to put any such notions firmly out of my mind.

Security, he reminded me, was relaxed for all officer prisoners while receiving treatment in hospital on the tacit understanding that, in return, they were deemed to have given their parole and, whilst they were there, no escape would be assayed. If I made an attempt and succeeded the Germans would be bound to take the view that a British officer's parole was worthless and, if past experiences were anything to go by, dire consequences in the form of ferocious restrictions would fall on all those ill and ailing comrades I left behind.

If, on the other hand, I failed . . . the Major shook his head slowly. What would happen to me then just wouldn't bear thinking about.

No, there were only two ways out of hospital. Three, if you counted going out as a corpse in a coffin. The first was - health restored - returning to a kriegie's life in the camp. The other was by medical repatriation, being shipped out of the camp and sent back to England on medical grounds.

I was suddenly very interested in those words: medical repatriation. How did that work?

The Major told me that every so often badly injured or very sick prisoners were exchanged on a one-for-one basis between Britain and Germany. In fact it was likely that, within the next two or three months, a neutral medical commission would be making the rounds of the camp hospitals to select - out of all the deserving cases - those who should be sent home.

My interest sagged instantly. How could I possibly ever be

judged injured enough or sick enough to qualify? Even if, by some miracle, I did, wouldn't I be denying the opportunity of going home to someone who really *needed* that trip more than me?

But the Major didn't stop there. He told me that the neutral medical commission frequently found it difficult to match the number of prisoners the British authorities were proposing for a particular one-for-one exchange. It had happened the last time, he told me. And it had happened here. The commission had really been forced to scrape the bottom of the barrel to make up the numbers. Quite a few technically undeserving cases had been nodded through and gone home.

This sounded almost too fanciful to be true. But, if it was true, why shouldn't I be one of those who got away? We talked for a long time, Major Matthews and I, and he agreed to help me stay in hospital until we could see whether history would be repeated.

To stay in hospital for two or three months I needed a substantial deterioration in my condition, and it was agreed that, as a first step, I would have to start vomiting again to convince the German doctor in charge that it was not yet time to transfer me back to the camp. Major Matthews suggested I should take an emetic every morning just before he came round with the German doctor. So on the pretence of visiting the lavatory I would sneak into the kitchen when the Russians had vacated it and mix myself a quick drink of warm water and a lot of salt - enough to make me vomit on the ward for all to see.

Each day the German doctor would be concerned that I had brought up my meagre breakfast and that this daily vomiting was sapping my strength. After that all I wanted to do was bury myself under the bed sheet and sleep. This went on day after day, week after week as I got weaker and weaker. From the outset it struck me as somehow ironic that a German doctor should show such concern over the deterioration in my health. After all, I was just one patient among many. But he was a painstaking practitioner and a compassionate man.

He was young, blond, good looking with a command of the English language and over the few weeks we had known each other he had seemed to develop a kind of friendly feeling for me. But, more than ever, when Major Matthews told me his story I couldn't understand why.

He'd had two brothers, one an army officer in a Panzer division and the other a medical man, and both had been involved in the Battle of Stalingrad, one of the bitterest and bloodiest battles of the entire war. Hitler had gambled on taking the city before the onset of the cruel Russian winter, to face which his troops were inadequately equipped. But it was a gamble he lost. The Russian defenders, though encircled and outnumbered, contested every street, every house, every ruin and every heap of battle-torn bricks.

They took everything General von Paulus could throw against them and they inflicted horrendous casualties on his Sixth Army. And they held the Germans in check until that same ally who had beaten Napoleon arrived, General Winter, closely followed by fresh, relieving Russian divisions which cut the German army in two and began a piecemeal slaughter.

Hitler had categorically refused to allow his troops to fight their way out of encirclement and retreat to safety. They were to fight and die where they stood. In the end, what was left of the German Sixth Army, ninety thousand frost-bitten and wounded men out of a total original strength of more than a quarter of a million, were forced to surrender and marched east on foot to Siberia, one of my doctor's brothers among them. Tens of thousands died on the way.

The other brother, both legs blown off in battle, was believed to have been evacuated by air before the end.

But this was only one part of the doctor's personal tragedy, Just a foretaste of worse things to come.

Major Matthews had found out that the doctor's wife lived in Hamburg and that she had been there when the RAF had carried out its series of assaults on the city - codenamed *Operation Gomorrah.* The first, on July 24 1943, was bad enough when seven hundred and ninety-one bombers dropped a greater tonnage of high explosive and incendiary bombs in three hours than the Luftwaffe had delivered to London in the five heaviest raids of the Blitz.

That night, for the loss of only twelve bombers, half the city was set alight and over fifteen hundred German civilians were killed.

The next night and the night after, the RAF came back again, with the US Eighth Air Force stoking up the flames with daylight raids in between. But it was the RAF assault on the fourth night, July 28th, which really opened up Hell's furnace door.

It lasted only forty-three minutes, but in that time nearly two thousand five hundred tons of bombs went down and, among them, was a lethal percentage of phosphorous incendiaries. It was a warm night with a gentle breeze blowing and all the ingredients were there for a totally new creation in the air war: fire-storm.

The burgeoning flames sucked in more and more air which rose swiftly when heated, only to be sucked in again to cyclonic effect. Round and round it went, rotating faster and faster with a terrible howling. Temperatures went straight off the scale. Whole streets, and the people in them, simply exploded into flame. Driven on by the wind, the fire-storm burned out nine square miles of the city in an eight hour inferno and, by the morning, forty-two thousand German civilians were dead.

The Germans, who had sown the wind in their terror raid on Coventry nearly three years before, had reaped the whirlwind.

The doctor's wife had survived the raid by a miracle, though their house had ceased to exist. But she miscarried as a result and lost the much hoped-for child which they had been expecting.

How that young German doctor in Stalag-Luft III, who had suffered so many personal tragedies at enemy hands, could show any vestige of compassion or concern for a bomber crew prisoner-of-war is past my comprehension. The fact that he did affects me emotionally, even to this day.

He was surely a true Christian. It was the doctor's active concern and the surreptitious advice given to me by Major Matthews that guaranteed my prolonged stay in hospital. Gradually as I got weaker with the daily routine of vomiting, I became completely detached from any contact with the other inmates in the ward and slept and dozed most of the day and night. The sheet was always drawn up over my head except when I stirred to make my morning visit to the kitchen, so that to all intents and purposes I was a corpse lying there.

While I was in this comatose state Wing Commander Stanford Tuck was admitted to the ward from the north compound. Like his friend Douglas Bader, he was one of our war heroes having shot down a record number of enemy planes, before his extraordinary luck ran out and he finished behind the wire. Tuck enquired the name of the corpse in the corner and was told "Oh. He's the 'dormouse' he's in his winter hibernation!" I never spoke to Tuck and I regret that I never surfaced to make a closer acquaintance.

The Germans also had their top fighter aces, the most distinguished being Major Adolph Galland who had excelled all others in his exploits in the air. He visited the compound at Stalag-Luft III just before I was admitted to hospital. I was told that he came strutting in wearing his Iron Cross full of teutonic arrogance, his entourage fawning around him. We didn't care for him much. But he must have had a good point or two since after the war he became a close friend of Douglas Bader and visited England frequently on business.

While in hospital I had no news of the progress of the Wooden Horse, but was deeply shocked to hear of the fate that befell many of those involved in another tunnelling operation which was later immortalised as *'The Great Escape'*.

A tunnel had been successfully excavated from under a hut in the north compound and at night eighty officers made their way out of the camp. A mass escape of such magnitude had never before been engineered in the history of prisoner-of-war camps. As Stalag-Luft III at Sagan was deep inside German occupied territory, the prisoners had decided to make for nearby Czechoslovakia, hoping that they might find support there as the people were very restive under the German occupation. By sheer coincidence, at the same moment, that widespread unrest came to the boil and the Germans, fully stretched on all fighting fronts, had their hands full trying to control a civilian uprising.

Unfortunately they immediately jumped to the conclusion that there was some sinister connection between the British prisoners' escape and the trouble in Czechoslovakia; that both had been master-minded by British agents. Nazi ruthlessness now knew no bounds.

The escaped officers were rounded up in an unprecedented country-wide search operation and shot under the guise of 'resisting arrest'. It was obvious that not all the fifty prisoners who were arrested in two's and three's would have put up any resistance when cornered by the security forces.

The whole of the camp at Sagan was shocked and angered at this inhuman conduct and the way the Germans had flouted the common laws of humanity as well as those of the Geneva Convention. The Senior British Officer demanded that he be allowed to inspect the bodies before burial but the request was ignored.

Apparently, soon after recapture, the murdered officers had been taken in several lorries into the nearby forest where they were ordered to alight, and were immediately mown down by the troops who had been escorting them. The crime was directed by the Gestapo who had refused to hand over the captured prisoners to the custody of senior officers of the Luftwaffe, despite their insistence that the prisoners were their responsibility.

It is documented in the archives of the Imperial War

Museum (which I have researched) that the Gestapo agents and the Nazi Generals who were responsible for this atrocity were sentenced to death by the Allied War Crimes Tribunal. So thorough was the Allied investigation that it was possible to name the men who had actually fired the fatal bullets, and they did not escape just retribution.

The Luftwaffe and, to give him his due, Von Lindeiner, the German Camp Commandant, was totally appalled by what had happened and official permission was readily given for the prisoners in Sagan to build their own memorial to the memory of their brave comrades. It was erected in the clearing in the forest just outside the camp confines: a forest clearing much like the one in which the escapees were murdered. It was constructed of stone, by the kriegies themselves, a truly noble memorial which would have done credit to any professional monumental stonemasons.

In the course of the next few weeks, the kits of all the murdered officers were auctioned off in the camp and raised £11,000 for their next of kin.

After all this upheaval in the life of the camp, the basic business of survival took on an added urgency for the rest of us. In the hospital my weeks of hibernation stretched into months as I became gradually weaker and weaker from the daily vomiting. Frequently, I would ask myself whether I was doing this to survive, or simply give myself a slow and lingering death sentence, but there was no going back.

When my resolve was being tested to the limit, there at last came some encouraging news. The neutral Medical Commission was due to visit Sagan, and my preoccupation then was to enlist Major Matthews' help to get my name on the list to be considered for repatriation on medical grounds. Before the Commission's arrival the German doctor arranged that, together with others, I should be taken by ambulance to Sagan's military hospital on the outskirts of the town, where I was to be X-rayed in an effort to diagnose the cause of my condition.

Major Matthews rose to the occasion, and advised me that if I were to swallow some small pellets of silver paper before the X-ray the radiologist would diagnose ulcers if the pellets got to the right place at the right time. For a doctor to tell a patient how to hoodwink a radiologist might seem entirely unethical but it proved Major Matthews was a soldier too and that he was only carrying out his duty, as a prisoner, to assist others to escape, even if he - by his calling, his rank and his own choice - was denied that opportunity for himself.

When the day for the trip to the military hospital arrived, Major Matthews was there in charge of the group of patients selected for screening accompanied by a German officer and the usual squad of armed guards. After a short ride, the ambulance drew up by the hospital entrance and, as Major Matthews was assisting the more immobile prisoners inside, he slipped me, as prearranged, three very small silver paper pellets which he had delicately manufactured from the lining of a cigarette packet.

I swallowed them surreptitiously once I was sure I was not being observed. They slipped down readily enough, though tension made my mouth very dry. The crunch was imminent. Where would the pellets show up when I was called to the X-ray room?

The hospital was in something of a turmoil, for seldom if

ever had it been called on to accommodate such a fair sized group of prisoners-of-war and their guards. Its facilities were stretched to the limit simply dealing with German casualties from the Russian front who needed X-rays for combat injuries to heads, legs and arms.

The English prisoners were pushed to one side while the Germans received preferential treatment which was only to be expected. We could only sit around and wait, grateful for the brief respite which the trip afforded from the confines of the hospital in the camp. It was a blessing to be out beyond the barbed wire.

For the more seriously injured in our group it was a frustrating time, naturally, but eventually the staff got around to dealing with us and slowly as each man returned from examination, he was quizzed anxiously by the others as to how he had fared. What precisely had happened? What questions had been asked?

The near universal report was that the bloody old fool in there had said that there was nothing seriously wrong. The bloody old fool being the examining German doctor. As my compatriots were visibly injured and visibly suffering, it did little to lift my spirits, particularly as Major Matthews had warned me that even if we were successful in having ulcers diagnosed, the condition might not be considered serious enough to warrant repatriation. At last, with trepidation, I was ushered into the X-ray room to be confronted with an alert but small pernickety old doctor who took his time, and was not in any way affected by the rush and bustle all around him.

He pummelled and prodded my stomach and concluded his examination of the X-ray plates by enquiring how long I had been suffering from the symptoms. As I was feeling very tense, weak and under the weather and my back had started playing up again it was not too difficult to act the invalid and, in a tremulous voice, I told him of my daily vomiting and the fact that I couldn't keep any food down inside me. He was quite uncommunicative, but although he hadn't given me any encouragement he hadn't given me the thumbs down and dismissed me as a phoney.

As we left the hospital, mostly sadder than when we had arrived, I felt a glimmer of hope, but we all kept very quiet as we knew that walls, particularly in these parts, had ears and that some of those walls understood English.

Then it was back to the old routine, there could be no relaxing under the eye of the young German doctor in the camp hospital. The daily, distressing vomiting sessions went on as we waited for the medical report from the military hospital.

It arrived within a week and - Hallelujah! - my name was on the list to be submitted to the Repatriation Commission. My condition had been confirmed as ulcers in the stomach. It was unbelievable. After four years of being treated like a cooped-up animal, I began tentatively to look forward to the possibility of release from a kriegie's trials and tribulations, now being exacerbated by an even more acute shortage of food within the camps and hard for my comrades to bear.

It was difficult to keep exhilaration in check but as I looked around at the serious condition of some of my fellow patients, with terrible burns and amputations, I appreciated the significance of Dr Matthew's warning, that ulcers alone might not prove sufficient to guarantee me a ticket to freedom. So when the time finally arrived for me to face the Repatriation Commission I realised that this was to be the most important day of my life.

This day would decide whether I could shake off the shackles of four years incarceration and once more be free. The stark alternative was that having punished my body very severely to get so far, if I failed this last hurdle I might not be able to survive the rigours of the camp for yet another winter. I must make a supreme effort to impress the Commission with my chronic incapacity.

Before my name was called I managed to struggle down to the kitchen which, as usual, was empty immediately after breakfast. I filled a tumbler half full with salt and quickly topped it up with water. Unfortunately there was insufficient water to dissolve all of the salt and, suddenly, there were footsteps approaching. So I drank up what I could and rapidly shovelled the rest of the salt down my throat with my fingers.

The result was instantaneous and dramatic, I felt so ill I could hardly stand. A Russian came in and eyed me curiously. I was sweating profusely. I literally staggered back to my bed where I pulled the sheet up over my head and prayed to God to help me through the day.

When the medical orderly arrived to take me before the inquisition I was almost unconscious and could only reel into the room with the orderly's support. Top ranking German military men resplendent in gold-braided uniforms bedecked with row upon row of medals, medical experts and officials of the International Red Cross were seated at the top of a boardroom sized table, while at the other end were the camp doctor and Major Matthews. The German Chairman of the

Commission looked as though he had seen a ghost as I almost fell into the seat in front of him. Major Matthews told me afterwards that he couldn't believe his eyes. I was not white. I was plain green. Everybody seemed aghast at my appearance.

My medical report was hurriedly read aloud and Major Matthews was asked to elaborate on my condition.

He was professional and concise explaining that the daily vomiting had sapped my strength and in the absence of the proper drugs to treat me, there was little hope for my survival. My X-ray plates were passed dutifully from one to another without comment. Some members obviously could interpret them, others pretended to do so. The Chairman focused on me, with the solemnity of a judge about to pass the death sentence, and in guttural but quite clear English pronounced the words I thought I would never hear "You shall go home!"

I received his verdict with no sign of emotion, but inside me was turmoil: elation and utter exhaustion each falling over the other.

With the orderly's help, I staggered back to the ward and slumped into bed where, in a comatose condition, with the sheet drawn over my head, those unbelievable words "You shall go home!" echoed and re-echoed throughout my brain. Then I was quickly asleep, dreaming of another world outside the confines of a prison camp.

Next day Major Matthews was jubilant at the success of the operation but, for us both, it was jubilation tempered with caution. The actual date of repatriation was still some months ahead and details had yet to be finalised as to the number which would be exchanged. We could only hope.

Meanwhile I had to continue to hoodwink the young

German doctor daily. I could not stage a sudden recovery as a result of hearing those magic words. Fortunately this last period of living a lie was mercifully brief as the Germans seemed anxious to get the exchange underway, and we were moved to a reception centre to facilitate our departure from Germany. Two thousand very ill, seriously crippled, blind and brain damaged cases were herded together in conditions I totally failed to foresee.

The sane and the insane, the mobile and the immobile were all pitched in together in complete and utter confusion.

11

Repatriation

IT WAS NOT THE HAPPY OCCASION I thought it would be, despite the prospect of going home. Most people seemed depressed and, when you thought about it, you could see why. A lot of those who surrounded me were cruelly disfigured. Some with their lips burned away, their ears burned off, eyelids non-existent so that they slept like corpses with eyes wide open . . . these were the ones who had been rescued from blazing aircraft, 'lucky to be alive'.

Many of the chronic sick had long since reached the end of their tether and it was certain that some of those who had heard those joyful words "You shall go home" would never survive the journey. And for those who did, what kind of welcome from their loved ones could they expect? A joyful reunion or a desperately disguised look of horror and utter revulsion?

Rumours abounded in the camp. D-Day, the 6th of June, had come and gone and Allied forces had landed in Europe. With our own eyes we could see increased bomber activity in the air. They flew high, the Superfortresses, in aerial armadas, ranging far and wide across Occupied Europe and German communications by road and by rail were chaotic. One day the rumour was that we were to be taken out of Germany via the South of France; the next day it was to be via Spain; but we still stayed put, we didn't move anywhere and depression grew. Eventually, the Red Cross arranged our exit through neutral Sweden and we were on the move.

On this final journey through Germany to the port of Stettin we travelled again in those familiar cattle trucks but, with the Red Cross supervising the move, we were shown more compassion than we had previously known in our brushes with this form of transport. From inside our trucks we could see little of the countryside, but as the train entered Berlin it came to an abrupt stop in what had been Templehof Station as an air raid warning had sounded. In the early days of the war, everybody who operated over Germany knew that Templehof airfield was the home of crack top-line squadrons, a first class fighter station. I had only heard of it then, never seen it, and I did not see it now. It had been bombed out of existence.

The runways alongside the railway track were overgrown. Everywhere was desolation. Bushes and brambles were taking over the railway station itself and I saw rabbits scurry along cracked and crazed platforms where previously crowds of businessmen had hurried and jostled to catch their trains.

The whole of the city had been laid flat. As far as the eye could see there was not one single building which had escaped. Blocks where factories and workshops had once been now sprouted tangled forests of twisted metal. Silence reigned supreme.

For the last year or more, in Sagan, we had seen the bombers of the American 8th Airforce heading for Leipzig and Dresden, so high up they appeared no larger than flashing pinheads. Such sights had revived our flagging spirits as we realised that those thousands of scintillating fireflies were Allied planes penetrating with impunity deep into the heart of the Reich. To us it was a scene of man-made beauty as the planes laid iridescent vapour trails like silver ribbons across the sky.

We had no idea then of the destruction those planes were about to wreak. Now, at close quarters, we were surveying the result of such handiwork, a result never known to the crews who dropped their bombs and returned as quickly as possible back home. The desolation defied description.

I realised that I had been fortunate in not having been able to actually see the destruction and death caused by the bombs we so happily dropped on our operations.

Germany was now reaping the whirlwind, but this was no time for sorrow or sympathy as we looked around at our mutilated companions and recalled the recent fate of those fifty of our comrades so brutally murdered by the Gestapo.

The German was still our enemy. He still gloated over the destruction of Coventry and London and we could have been excused if we'd had the stomach to gloat over Berlin.

Stettin was the light we were looking for in the depths of this gloom and it appeared at last, in the form of gaunt, grey, wet and dreary dockland. Nevertheless our spirits stirred in the knowledge that the long and tedious train journey was over.

It was a slow and painful business transferring the desperately injured aboard the ferries, but when it was done and the ferries cast off we were safe in the hands of the International Red Cross. We had been mercifully delivered from captivity in Germany, but only a few of us were active enough to physically express the overwhelming relief we all felt in our hearts.

It was a short and pleasant trip across the narrow straits to Trelleborg in Sweden, the promised land, where we again entrained, but this time in comfort, for Gothenburg. Here we were accommodated not far from the dockyard, in a school which had been very comfortably converted to meet our requirements. While awaiting the arrival of two large Red Cross hospital ships we were given a hero's welcome by the Swedes who had managed to stay neutral throughout the war.

We were guarded by young Swedish airforce cadets who were thrilled to be rubbing shoulders with battle-hardened British RAF officers who had survived the ordeal of being shot down and interned for years in enemy camps. They were just starting out on their flying careers, and begged us for souvenirs. We had little to give, but they accepted the buttons we tore off our uniforms with as much enthusiasm as if they had been made of gold.

On the first evening we were entertained royally by a reception committee of English speaking Swedish ladies who had brought their beautiful daughters with them. Before the war there had been a constant movement of ships between Stockholm and Gothenburg and the Humberside ports in England and the Swedish seamen, like their predecessors the Vikings, had carried many a pretty maiden back to Sweden to wed. Their daughters after frequent visits to their English grandparents were as much English as they were Swedish and spoke both languages fluently. Mothers and daughters all welcomed us as excitedly as though we were long lost sons and brothers returning home.

We had forgotten over the years what a table looked like covered with fine linen and silver and mouth-watering food. The sight outdid the Lord Mayor's Banquet in our estimation. The Red Cross doctors had warned us about the dangers of over-indulging our appetites after the near starvation diet we had endured in the camps. Our digestions, they warned, would be unable to cope. But such warnings fell on deaf ears where many of the prisoners were concerned. My stomach however had not only contracted, it had become very painful, and I found my thoughts less concerned with gluttony than, looking around me, with another of the seven deadly sins.

It is hard to appreciate the life we had led for four years, deprived even of the sight of a pretty woman, and there we were now surrounded by comely women with daughters so lovely that we were momentarily struck dumb. At first we were like shy public schoolboys being introduced to their female counterparts from a nearby academy for young ladies and many of the prisoners were too sick mentally and physically to have the close proximity of so much feminine pulchritude arouse the old Adam. The rest of us were soon chattering like starlings. But not for long.

All of us rapidly found that our fund of polite, civilised conversation was easily exhausted. We had lived apart from the real world for too long to find the road back could be travelled in a few hours. It was painfully apparent that not only would our bodies need loving care and repair but also our mental muscles would require exercise and our psychic and spiritual energies a dynamic recharge. The truth was that we had come out of the camps broken in body and mentally and spiritually exhausted.

That night I slept in a comfortable bed with clean sheets. Next morning two gleaming white hospital ships painted with huge red crosses on their sides, decks and funnels were awaiting us in the docks. We had been up at the crack of dawn, had experienced the forgotten luxury of a soak in a hot bath and were soon the target of Swedish and international photographers.

The more active and daring of us had photos taken with pretty Swedish nurses sitting on our knees. After years of monastic celibacy we were conscious of shivers of excitement as we made even this restricted contact with the warm female bodies of our companions, posing with us for the cameras. I was soon reassured that the flame I feared malnutrition might have extinguished in me forever would be easily and quickly reignited given the right opportunity.

The time came all too quickly for us to say our affectionate farewells as we filed on to the hospital ships; I thought I detected a tear in the eye of my very friendly young Swedish nurse. I know I had a lump in my throat as we kissed goodbye.

A band struck upon the pier and there was much frantic waving and cheering as, with the quiet dignity befitting floating hospitals, the ships slid silently away from Sweden. Those in charge of them were well aware that, despite the fact that they had been promised safe passage because of the nature of their mission of mercy, this voyage to England was to be no pleasure cruise. The war was still raging. The seas everywhere were heavily mined.

While in Swedish waters, the ships had the guidance and

protection of Swedish naval patrol vessels. After a day and night steaming quietly north we were picked up by German torpedo boats off Norway, which accompanied us close inshore against a backdrop of an inhospitable coastline. High mountains were riven by deep fiords, invitingly calm when viewed from our tossing and heaving decks.

Below decks, accommodation on our ships was very limited so, whenever they could, the mobile prisoners lay out in the open soaking up the weak sunshine and enjoying the fresh air. Around us patrol boats kept station whilst, overhead, fighter aircraft swooped low to catch a glimpse of the floating hospitals silently progressing through the turbulent waters.

Then, as the two ships dramatically altered course away from the protective coastline and swung out into the wide expanse of the North Sea, the German torpedo boats turned back. And with dusk came a damp grey mist over the water and rougher seas.

Our ships were not blacked out. Light blazed down on the giant red crosses and one brief visit to the wet and slippery deck provided a fleeting glimpse of a surfaced U-boat taking a closer look at us as we battled by. It resembled a huge lethargic hippo as the rough seas parted momentarily and then ran as foaming rivulets down its black shining sides before it plunged down again into the murky depths.

It was a unique experience in wartime to be standing on the deck of a ship and seeing one of these lethal enemy monsters without going in fear of imminent death. It was not powerless to strike, far from it. But we were blessed with the protection of those huge red crosses from this predator of international sea lanes.

The next surprise was to be suddenly buzzed by British reconnaissance aircraft as they streaked at unbelievable speed in an explosion of sound low over the water then rose and dipped their wings in salute before disappearing, their RAF roundels flashing in the early light. It was incredible. When we had first been imprisoned, naval biplanes had been used for reconnaissance at sea. We had never seen such sleek machines at close quarters, flying at such an amazing speed. We realised then that we, like the early wartime aircraft we had so proudly flown, were now in fact obsolete. Time had marched on.

The presence of these British planes made us think we were nearly home. We were in fact in Arctic waters around Greenland!

Allied convoys were still ploughing their way along these sea routes to Murmansk and it was towards this promising area that the German U boat we had seen earlier before was carefully edging its way, very conscious of the presence of British naval patrols and aircraft. The sea was still covered in a murky mist, through which the weak yellow rays of the sun shone intermittently to give a ghostly look to the area which had become the graveyard of so many Allied merchant ships and their gallant crews.

It was to avoid convoys and the murderous German wolfpack attacks upon them that we had been routed so far to the north. But eventually the news which we had awaited so long finally came through. We were nearing Liverpool and would dock the next day.

Home at last. It was unbelievable!

The evacuation of the ships was a military exercise. No

visitors were allowed. No bands played a welcome home. It was the antithesis of everything that had happened in Sweden.

Fresh troops were embarking daily for the war still raging in Europe and in the Far East and the arrival of casualties from the battlefronts was an everyday occurrence. To the dockworkers we were just normal human cargo destined for hospitalisation. A few photographers recorded the arrival of the Red Cross hospital ships for the War Office photofiles and we were quietly whisked away to a large RAF hospital at Weeton near Blackpool - a ragged smelly bunch of casualties who everyone appeared anxious to be rid of.

Medical inspections began early next morning and nurses were bustling briskly around the wards switching on lights and pulling recalcitrant sleepers from their beds to get the day started. Some of the mentally unstable prisoners, who hardly realised where they were, stood rigidly by their beds swearing threateningly at anyone who came near them. The doctors were unable to placate them and the poor overworked nurses must have been at their wits' end.

Such patients were eventually dealt with sympathetically, tranquilised, and despatched to appropriate centres where, hopefully, they could be restored to health. But their initial violent reaction to the medical staff was to pose a problem for me.

Everyone wore a metal dog-tag round his neck which had been issued by the German medical authorities and which carried the reason for his repatriation. But most of the mental patients were insisting there was nothing at all wrong with them and saying so in an abusive, threatening and violent manner. The snag was that as I had been repatriated as a result of intrigue, I could quite legitimately claim that there really was nothing wrong with me, but the more often I said it the less I was believed.

When the English doctor who was interviewing me and who obviously didn't understand enough German to read the diagnosis on my tag asked what was the matter with me, I replied perhaps a little truculently "Nothing at all!"

This was precisely the reply being given by most of the mental patients, and it took me some time to convince the doctor that my story of intrigue, the escape plan I had hatched and carried out with the assistance of Doctor Matthews, wasn't just a figment of a gravely disordered mind.

Pending further investigation, I was given the benefit of the doubt and left in the ward and not hastily removed to a mental hospital.

A few days of relaxation followed, then I was ordered to appear before a medical board to tell my story and to explain why, when there was seemingly not much wrong with me, I had been medically repatriated.

At the end of the interrogation, the Chairman of the Board turned to his neighbour and asked incredulously "Do you think we would have been taken in like that?"

"Quite possibly," was the dry reply.

After much deliberation it was concluded that the large doses of salt I had ingested had taken the lining off my stomach, which could not therefore properly carry out the digestive process. Daily doses of weak hydrochloric acid were prescribed and I was instructed to play golf daily on the local green as part of my rehabilitation.

The war was still on and I found playing golf a little

inappropriate, so I eventually managed to get myself posted to light duty and found myself at RAF Lyneham, a Transport Command station.

Incredulously, on arrival I learned I was to be trained as a Traffic Control officer. I had been shot down in 1940 when communications technology was in its infancy, and after four years in limbo was being pitchforked straight into a highly sophisticated electronic environment. The fevered activity in the control tower, bringing in planes to land while holding others in safe sectors until their turn came, was indescribable. Phones were ringing, radio messages were crackling over the air, blips and flashes filled the radar screens, I had found myself in a modern tower of Babel!

I promptly advised a very sympathetic station commander that this didn't suit me at all and unless I quickly got a transfer to something I understood I really would be a candidate for the funny farm.

In fact, the day before I left Lyneham I thought the new posting might have come too late and that the cacophonous confusion of the control tower might just have tipped me over the edge.

I was up there, saying my fond farewells, when a large transport plane returned from a trip to Egypt and rolled slowly along the runway until it disappeared from view over a slight rise. Within minutes of disappearing, everybody in the control tower was amazed to see a large, scraggy, mangy camel come trotting back down the runway towards the tower. The young exuberant crew had thought it would be a great joke to bring this ship of the desert back to Lyneham and to see how the airfield control staff would deal with such a contingency.

Fortunately or unfortunately, I was not in Lyneham long enough to hear the eventual fate of the camel, whether it had to be repatriated, or whether it supplemented the station's meagre meat ration.

My next, and more suitable, posting turned out to be as assistant to the Adjutant at RAF Madley, where I was still in residence when the war in Europe came to a sudden end in May 1945 and I was transferred to RAF Cosford to assist in the reception of hundreds of RAF officers being flown home from prison camps in Germany.

I had often seriously wondered whether all the damage I had inflicted on my stomach had been worthwhile, when the only achievement, at first sight, had been the remission of a mere eight months of captivity before the war's end. But, at Cosford, I was quickly reassured that it had been.

There I had to deal with some of my close associates from Stalag-Luft III and I could hardly believe that their condition could have deteriorated so much in such a relatively short time. But as soon as the Nazis had finally realised that defeat was not only inevitable but imminent they had driven their prisoners out on to the roads in forced marches to keep them ahead of the advancing Allies, hoping to use them as hostages or bargaining counters. And these marches had taken a very heavy toll.

Those survivors arriving at Cosford were emaciated and exhausted, and many told horror stories of comrades who could not contend with marches of up to twenty or more miles in a day and died at the roadside when so near to salvation.

I heard this again and again.

I was still at Cosford in September 1945 when I was called

before a demobilisation board. As I had suffered some injuries during my service I was assessed to see whether such injuries would warrant my being granted any kind of a disability pension from a grateful Government. The X-ray examination which followed, I was told, confirmed that my back injury had resulted in two vertebrae at the base of the spine being fused together. The head injury showed as a thickened area of bone at the base of the skull where a fracture had mended over a period of time.

One of the doctors conducting the assessment had the courtesy to ask whether I had recently experienced any adverse effects from my injuries, which was a welcome change from the cavalier attitude adopted by his colleagues, who were prepared to dismiss them as being of no account. I replied in all sincerity: "Well, whenever I laugh I experience quite a severe pain at the base of my skull, which develops into a very bad headache."

The response from the bluff Chairman of the Board was succinct, if unsympathetic in the circumstances. "Well that won't be a problem in the future. You are now returning to Civvy Street, and you'll have precious little to laugh at there!"

In retrospect I am glad that so many people were more fulsome in their appreciation of the efforts of the RAF, those lucky enough to have survived, and those who sadly had to give their all. Most people in England are still, after all these many years, ready to echo those immortal words of Winston Churchill: "Never in the field of human conflict was so much owed by so many to so few".

That Chairman of the Board might not agree but I'd like him to know that contrary to his cynicism I have found lots to laugh at during forty and more years back in Civvy Street.

I would add that it's great to be still alive and active at the fairly ripe, but young, age of 79 years as I finish this story, which I attribute to being blessed with a most marvellous wife, two caring children and four charming grandchildren to all of whom I have dedicated this account of some of the episodes in my wartime life.

About the Author

Born in 1910, 'Ollie' Oliver grew up on Lord Cholmondley's Estate, where his father was Gamekeeper and whenever he spoke of his childhood he evoked a way of life gone forever. They were long summer days on the great estate with its armies of gardeners and servants and horse-drawn ploughs. Days spent learning to fish and ride and shoot with his father, or plucking pheasants, jugging hare or making jam with his mother. Here was born that love of nature and country ways which never left him.

But despite his roots in the countryside, he was fascinated by the City and joined Barclays DCO when it was *the* international bank and was posted to Trinidad where, with servants to attend every whim and the marvellous weather, life for a good looking bachelor was, as he used to say, 'truly paradise'.

But on September 3rd 1939 his life changed dramatically.

Britain and Germany went to war and Ollie couldn't stay out of it. Within days he'd booked passage home to volunteer for the RAF and he flew with No. 78 and No. 10 Squadron until being shot down over Italy.

For the next four years he was a prisoner, but never for one single instant did he stop trying to escape. Finally, by dint of an extraordinary and most dangerous subterfuge, he was returned to England in late 1944 and actively served in the RAF until the war's end. In 1946, back with Barclays, he returned to Trinidad, where he married, had children and stayed until 1960. In 1963, he was appointed Barclays' Company Secretary and retired in 1971.

He enjoyed a very active retirement. At an age when many people slow down, he was still busy gardening, dashing to auctions in pursuit of his art interests, fishing, flying to his beloved Spain and writing books. (He was 79 when he wrote this one).

He loved life and he loved people. He was 85 when the Grim Reaper, who had so narrowly missed him on that wartime night over Italy, finally caught up with him again.

By all who knew him, he is still very fondly remembered.

Museum of Allied Prisoners of War Martyrdom in Sagan (Żagań)

During the Second World War, the Germans built a number of PoW camps in and around Sagan (Żagań in Polish). All except one were camps for military prisoners and were governed by the 8th Military District of the Wehrmacht. The exception was the camp called Stalag-Luft III, built in May 1942 and controlled directly by the High Command of the Luftwaffe.

At first, most of the prisoners held there were RAF officers and American pilots. Later, aircrew from virtually all of the Allied nations might be found there. In 1944, Stalag-Luft III housed over 10,000 prisoners.

The treatment of prisoners in the military Stalags varied from harsh and cruel to determinedly evil and inhumane. Stalag VIIIC at Sagan and its associated camp, Stalag VIIIE at Neuhammer (in Polish, Świętoszów) had a PoW population of over 100,000 at peak times but this figure dropped markedly as the deliberate extermination of the Russian inmates at Neuhammer got into its stride. Starvation, epidemics and beatings in all the military Stalags also took a heavy toll.

Conditions in Stalag-Luft III were better, possibly as a result of Luftwaffe control. On the debit side, from the German point of view, Luft III became notorious for its number of attempted escapes. The biggest of these was organised by a secret Escape Committee established in Spring 1943 and led by Major Roger Bushell. It took place on the night of 24 March 1944 when eighty prisoners got out of the camp in 'The Great Escape'.

After the alarm was raised, four prisoners were recaptured almost immediately. Seventy-three more were apprehended later and, in pursuance of Hitler's personal order - *Sagan Befehl* - fifty of these were subsequently murdered by the Gestapo . . . allegedly resisting arrest!

In 1947, eighteen of the murderers who had carried out Hitler's order faced a British Military Tribunal in Hamburg. Fourteen were sentenced to death by hanging (in the end only thirteen of them died) and the others received lengthy prison sentences. In contrast, most of the monsters who ordered and carried out the mass exterminations in Stalag VIIIC and its associated camps between 1942 and 1945 were never punished at all . . .

The Museum of Allied Prisoners of War Martyrdom in Żagań
stands as a permanent memorial to all those who suffered -
and those who died - in all these cruel camps.
The Museum is open:
daily from 10am to 4pm Tuesday - Friday
and 10am - 5pm on Saturday and Sunday.
It is closed on Mondays.

It is situated at: ul. Lotnikow Alianckich 9, 68-100, Żagań, on ground once occupied by Stalag VIIIC and nearby is the Memorial erected by their comrades to those prisoners of Stalag-Luft III so cruelly murdered by the Gestapo more than fifty long years ago.